Newsworld

Drue Heinz Literature Prize 2006

newsworld

Todd James Pierce

UNIVERSITY OF PITTSBURGH PRESS

Published by the University of Pittsburgh Press, Pittsburgh, PA 15260

Copyright © 2006, Todd James Pierce

Manufactured in the United States of America

Printed on acid-free paper

10 9 8 7 6 5 4 3 2 1

Library of Congress Cataloging-in-Publication Data

Pierce, Todd James, 1965-

   Newsworld / Todd James Pierce.

      p.   cm.

   "Drue Heinz Literature Prize 2006."

   ISBN 0-8229-4299-2 (cloth : alk. paper)

   1. United States—Social life and customs—Fiction. I. Title.

   PS3616.I36N49 2006

   813'.6—dc22   2006019187

CONTENTS

Columbine: The Musical   1

Wrestling Al Gore   21

Arise and Walk, Christopher Reeve   37

Newsworld   59

Studio Sense   87

Day of the Dead   101

The Real World   122

The Yoshi Compound: A Story of Post-Waco Texas   145

Sirens   174

Newsworld II   194

Acknowledgments   203

Newsworld

Columbine: The Musical

On Wednesday morning, between math and PE, I learned that Robbie Fenstermaker, who was set to play Dylan Klebold in our school's production of *Columbine: The Musical*, had wrecked a driver's training car and fractured his collarbone. "Collarbone?" repeated Mr. Baxter, my PE teacher. He combed his fingers through his sparse, aluminum-toned hair. "We're talking a good two months' recovery. More if it was a nasty break. When's this play set to open anyhow?"

"In a week and a half," I told him.

"Better scratch him off the program. He's not doing any acting for some time."

Here was my problem: I was Robbie's understudy. I knew some of his lines. I'd even practiced them with my girlfriend, Susan, who got a little turned on when I imitated Robbie's stage voice, but I never thought I'd need to play this role in the actual production. I was a quiet kid. I'd only tried out because Susan was in the play. I stood there dumbfounded, dressed in our school's PE uniform: blue shorts, gold jersey, my name, Greg Gorman, thickly inked across my chest. After the activity bell rang, Mr. Baxter sent us out for six laps while he settled into a beach chair and asked one of his female assistants to bring him a diet Coke.

With the other boys, I ran my laps around our school's new "safety" track—a quarter-mile circuit enclosed by a ten-foot fence topped with barbed wire. I generally did what I was told and believed this would be the key to my future success. I was good with directions, liked organization, never challenged the teachers or security officers at my school. For example, I was happy in my role as "Library Victim Number Four." I was good at feigning panic, good at singing the soft, low chorus of death we all sang lying on the floor while other students who played our parents walked through the library holding poster-sized reproductions of our dental records above their heads. I had no real ambition to be the star of anything, let alone our school play.

All morning long I told no one about Robbie's accident, not even Susan, who stood beside me in the lunch line. She was a tall girl with dark blond hair that fell in a straight line to her shoulders. On that day, she wore the Abercrombie leather necklace I'd bought for her as a three-month anniversary gift and a tank top that showed off her tan shoulders. Occasionally I wondered why she was going out with me at all—clearly football players were interested—but like me, her father had left her family when she was in junior high. I believed we shared something because of this, a certain hopefulness perhaps, though I can't say for sure what that was. When we got near the front of the line, she pushed through and ordered for us both. I had the same thing every day—a cheeseburger and Coke.

After Susan's father left, her mother had become an executive secretary for a law firm specializing in lucrative class-action suits filed by ex-smokers. My mother, on the other hand, experienced repeated episodes of road rage until she finally gave in to the beauty of a quasi-Eastern inner peace and enrolled at the community college to become a certified workplace counselor specializing in conflict management. Because of her, I'd found my own inner peace as well: I looked for the best in other people and had learned that the meaning of life was found in universal goodness. That is, I believed we were all basically good people just trying to get along, though sometimes because of our own flawed understanding of the world, we had trouble seeing how other people were trying their best to get along with us.

I spent the afternoon in history class, then in study hall, where I worked on my algebra homework, graphing parabolas that stretched toward infinity. After school, I stayed in the library long enough to miss the beginning of our daily rehearsal. As a rule I hated to be late for anything, but I hoped Mr. Sweeney would select someone else to take the role of Dylan Klebold if I wasn't there on time. Only when the library was about to close did I finally load my books into my mesh backpack—the type of backpack our vice principal had instructed all students to use at the beginning of the school year.

I arrived at the theater a good half hour late, my backpack slung over one shoulder, and sat on the outer steps next to a publicity poster for *Our Town*, the play Mr. Sweeney had directed the previous spring. Though he was interested in the "force of negative publicity," he had yet to put up posters for *Columbine: The Musical* because he was tired of local reporters stopping in to see how we were doing. Already one of these stories had been picked up by the wire service, a short column accompanied by the headline: "Whatever Happened to Hamlet?"

Through heavily tinted glass, I saw that the other students weren't rehearsing a scene, nor were they practicing the song "I Have a Gun, I Have an Arsenal" that Mr. Sweeney had rewritten over the weekend. Instead they were sitting on the bare stage in a circle, their hands joined, as Mr. Sweeney said how proud he was of them, his troupe of teenaged actors. "Musical theater has a message," he reminded us, "and that message is, 'Wake up, America! Hear the song the youth of your country is singing.'"

As always, Susan was sitting beside her friend Rosemary, who played Cassie Bernal, the Christian girl who died a martyr. She looked so pretty there, Susan did, with her hair pulled back, dressed in the thin, striped sweater she wore as part of her costume, complete with tear-away patches on the stomach and sleeve where Mr. Sweeney would hide blood-packs on the night of the actual performance. I watched her eyes move around the room and wondered if she was looking at other guys, but eventually her gaze settled on me. Or rather it settled on the tinted window beyond which I sat, as if she knew I was out there, resting on the steps.

For ten minutes, Mr. Sweeney went on about how this play would expose real-life violence as the means of entertainment it had become. I watched him walk across the stage, his hair pulled back into a ponytail, his black turtleneck tight enough to reveal a slight paunch, his hands gesturing in a certain William Shatner way whenever he got excited. When he was almost finished lecturing, I left my spot on the stairwell, slipped into the theater and leaned against the sound booth.

Mr. Sweeney stood center stage, next to a rack of plastic guns designed to look like the real thing. His gaze shifted to me, his eyes so blue most kids thought he wore colored contacts. Surely he knew how content I was as "Library Victim Number Four," lying deathly still while the students who played my parents carried me to the steel autopsy tables located in the side aisles of our theater. I did not have the ambition to take the role of Dylan Klebold, hell-bound follower of Eric Harris. Clearly Mr. Sweeney saw my reluctance, but what choice did he have? "Every great play has its own reckoning," he said. "No doubt this will be ours."

¤

After rehearsal Susan and I went to our lockers to get our books. Our lockers had new clear plastic doors so teachers could see what we kept inside them, though I kept nothing but notebooks and granola bars in mine. On our way out we nodded good-bye to our school detective, Officer Brubaker, who liked us so much he didn't make Susan walk through the metal detector again whenever something in her purse set it off.

Officially, Mr. Sweeney had told the school board he was producing a "musical to help students understand the effects of school violence," but we all believed this play would've been canned if our principal had not been on heavy chemo that semester. Even with this, Mr. Sweeney only got the green light once the SafeCampus Corporation agreed to sponsor the play, thereby giving our school a much-needed ten-percent discount on all the video cameras, see-through locker housings, and security fencing our vice principal had ordered that year.

In truth we all wanted something from this play. Susan wanted to get into an acting program at Rutgers. Mike Rogers, the boy who played Eric Harris, wanted to be a paid spokesperson for Youth Against Violence. Mr. Sweeney wanted critical attention so he could leave our school and direct revivals off-Broadway. As for me, I wanted to be with Susan as much as I could because we were both seniors. After graduating, I was planning to study business in college—Rutgers if possible—and after college, I wanted to manage a store at the mall. That is to say, I wanted to find a job like my father held before he fell in love with Loni the flight attendant and moved to Burma.

As we dumped our backpacks into the backseat of her car, Susan turned to me somewhat cautiously. Recently she had begun to treat me as though she were slightly older, more experienced. I never said anything about it. The best way to deal with trouble like this, I'd learned, was to push it away from you—to say to yourself, Self, I am not a perfect person either.

Once buckled in, she said, "You don't want to be Dylan Klebold, do you?"

"I'm not a good actor."

"Well don't you have all the luck? You don't even *want* a lead role and you end up being Dylan Klebold. I mean, *Dylan Klebold*. You get to carry around a gun. You shoot people. You look cool. Me? I get popped twice, then lie on the floor singing that stupid chorus of death for ten minutes."

"I like lying on the floor and singing that chorus of death."

"You like it because it's easy. You know, pop-pop, down you go. Anyone could do that. But Dylan Klebold. He's, like, super-wussie, patsy to the stars. It takes skill to play a role like that." She started her car, the engine catching on the second try. "God, why couldn't Rosemary run her car into a ditch?"

"You might regret saying that," I told her.

"Seriously, if I got to play Cassie, I'd be in Rutgers like you wouldn't believe. I'd be on scholarship. I'd be doing commercials on cable within three years. Mark my words, made-for-TV movies would be in my future."

We left the parking lot slowly since the street was heavily patrolled. We both checked for cops before passing a billboard our school boosters owned. "Remember, Kids," it said, "Stay Off Drugs!"

We spent the evening at Susan's house, just like we always did. She helped me practice the role of Dylan Klebold. Truthfully, the role wasn't as big as those of Cassie, or Eric Harris, or even Sheriff John Stone, but we both felt it was important in its own way, especially with its "Manhattan Monologue." In it, Klebold talks about his fantasy of hijacking a passenger jet and crashing it into Manhattan. On stage, while Robbie Fenstermaker—or rather while I—read this monologue, Mr. Sweeney planned to project slides from Klebold's and Harris's actual diaries onto a screen that dropped from the orchestra shell. At the same time, the students who played the eventual victims were to line up behind me and hum the soft, low chorus of future dread.

Without much prodding, Susan sensed my frustration. I was still speaking in my "Library Victim Number Four" voice. I couldn't seem to get beyond it, not even when I described the passenger jet as a "burning comet of hate" I would commandeer into Park Avenue. She pretended not to think poorly of me, but eventually clicked on the Playboy Channel. She told me, "Watching nude women will help you take hold of this role." We watched a segment called "Totally Naked Women Smoking Cigars" and part of a game show called "You Bet Your Clothes."

As usual, we ended up in her mother's four-poster bed with its faux-satin sheets. Since meeting Susan, I'd become much better at sex than I would've thought possible a year ago. On our second date she'd told me I was exceptionally well endowed, and on subsequent dates she began to teach me how to move in such a way as to better please her. By the time her mother got home, we were dressed again. Around her mother, I liked to pretend we weren't having sex, but Susan said her mother didn't really care about things like that, as long as she stayed on the pill.

I spent the rest of the night at home reading my lines out loud. I was doing my best to get words like "mother fucker" to sound right when I said them. I stood in front of my mirror and repeated the line, "All you asshole jocks must die!" but no matter how I said it, the lines lacked a certain youthful power and conviction I knew they required. I was good at enunciating all the syllables, but couldn't get my voice to project the right emotion, even when I took myself back, moment by moment, to the day my father left for Burma. He'd left a note on my dresser—a small piece of paper, folded in half. "Catch you later, Greg," it said. "P.S. Don't be a stranger."

¤

The next morning I woke at 5:30. I liked waking early because it gave me extra time to contemplate my life. Often I visualized my father, dressed in a red Hawaiian shirt, sitting beside me on my bed. Usually he said little words of encouragement, like, "I'm really proud of your algebra homework" or "Way to go on that Latin test, Greg!" I can't tell you how much these affirmations helped me get through a hard day of school. But on this particular morning, he sat silently, dressed in his red Hawaiian shirt, his hands folded into his lap. No matter how hard I tried, I couldn't visualize him saying anything. Eventually he removed an imaginary pack of smokes from his shirt pocket and lit one.

By 6:30 I was dressed in my gym clothes, ready to head off to school. "Something's different about you," my mother said. She was wearing one of her periwinkle blue suits. Periwinkle was one of the three recommended colors for certified workplace counselors specializing in conflict management.

"I have a new role in the school play."

She fixed me with her trained gray eyes. "You're going to knock them dead. I just know it."

As I jogged to school, I noticed the first advertisements for the play on telephone poles and in shop windows. They featured the title in an elegant copperplate script along with a small publicity photo of Mr. Sweeney wearing a black dinner jacket and bow tie. In the bottom margin was the SafeCampus logo, along with their slogan: "Because You Don't Really Know Who Lives Down the Street." By the time I reached school, I felt a certain dread settle into my stomach, a feeling I didn't know how to push aside, but after Officer Brubaker gave me the thumbs-up, I felt I owed it to myself to go about my morning just as I would any other.

I went immediately to our new "full-security" gym. By spring I hoped to have pecs and abs so developed that Susan wouldn't be embarrassed to be seen with me at the pool. After my first set of sit-ups, however, I couldn't concentrate. I kept thinking of my impending failure as Dylan Klebold, boy murderer. How would I ever fit my body into his? Twice I forgot how many reps I'd done on the bench press, and while racking dumbbells, I dropped one on my foot, a good fifteen pounds right across my toes. I was so upset and mad I had to sit on the floor and hold my injured foot in both hands. Only after my toes stopped throbbing did I glance into the two-way workout mirrors that lined the opposite wall. I almost didn't recognize my own face. My eyes were slits, my lips an angry line drawn above my chin. For the first time, I isolated a piece of the actual pain that Dylan Klebold must have felt, the first grain from which he formed his murderous beach.

"Mother Fucker," I said. I listened to my voice. It sounded good— as good as Robbie Fenstermaker's had sounded when he stood onstage holding a replica of a TEC-DC9 handgun with detachable metal clip. *"Mother Fucker,"* I said again. *"All you asshole jocks must die!"*

A boy straddling a free-weight bench turned to me. "Hey theater geek," he said, "shut your fat mouth."

¤

All morning I focused on this pain, the crunch of the dumbbell landing against my toes, how I crumpled on to the neoprene mats that padded the floor and held my foot. For a few moments I forgot about myself entirely. I forgot about the other people using the new "full-security" gym, I forgot about the cameras mounted to the four corners of the room. I was simply mad and hurt. To be honest, for one split second, I felt like hitting someone, but then I realized the power of this insight. I was given this moment of pain so I could *be* Dylan Klebold in our school's play.

Between classes, I practiced my new persona. I spoke with more force, issuing my desires as statements rather than as simple questions. "Please let me through to my locker," I said to a group of freshmen conversing in the breezeway. To our school's librarian, seated at her desk, I said, "I'm ready to check this book out." At lunch, with Susan, I held my own place in the cafeteria line and even pushed toward the window I felt would serve us the fastest.

We sat on the far edge of the lawn, Susan and I, just inside the ten-foot fence, amongst other kids involved with theater arts. She kept staring at me, her eyes narrowed, searching for the origins of my change, but I wanted to keep the exact cause of my transformation a secret. Its power came in part from its mystery. Eventually she sat next to me and touched her shoulder to mine. "You know what would be great," she said. "It'd be great to have some place to go for lunch. Like a friend's apartment. Someplace with a bed. I have all this stress from my morning classes, and I just want to let it out."

I focused again on the pain I'd felt that morning, that white-hot flash of irrational anger. I let my voice slide into the lower register so it sounded just like Robbie Fenstermaker's. "Let's ram this burning comet of hate into Park Avenue," I said.

She turned to me, her eyes swimming in desire. "Don't do that to me now," she said. "I'm horny enough as it is."

¤

That afternoon I asked my study hall monitor, Mrs. Glass, if I could practice my lines outside. I explained that I was now Dylan Klebold in our school's play, an important role, and that I only had a few days to memorize the lines. "Whatever," she said. "Just don't sit by the cameras. I don't need any more heat about kids ditching my class."

I sat outside the woodshop building, one of our school's camera-free zones—also a big druggie hangout. Under a maple tree I ran through those lines I didn't know by heart. I even began to stylize them in a way I thought appropriate to my character. I didn't just say, "Locked and loaded," like I would if I were "Library Victim Number Four." Instead I said, "Locked," then waited a moment before I came through with the expected close.

At rehearsal I was nervous again. I was aware how much more talented the other leads were compared to me. In the far corner, by the piano, Rosemary and Susan practiced their duet, "Calling Me Home." On stage, Ms. Jacobs, our choreographer, walked the students who played the victims' parents through the dance steps for the number, "When Hitler's Birthday Comes to a Small Town Like Ours."

At last I read through the "Manhattan Monologue," doing my best to become Dylan Klebold. "Let people throw rocks at me," I said. "Let them call me a wimp. We will all go down together. Then they will know how I felt—outcast, loser, a boy looking for someone to be his friend." I stood there silently, center stage, as a hoop of tangerine light dropped down around me; then Mike Rogers, who played Eric Harris, walked onstage. We gave each other our usual greeting, "Sieg heil," slapped hands and walked off together.

After rehearsal, I could tell Mr. Sweeney was impressed. He took me into his office—a small room at the back of the theater, furnished with two couches from the Goodwill and a desk. He patted me on the back and motioned for me to take a seat on the sofa opposite him. He held his hands before him, much in the classic manner of William Shatner, indicating he was about to say something important. "Earlier today I was worried," he confessed. "I thought I'd need to find someone else to play Klebold. I don't believe much in method acting. Typecasting is the practical way to go. But this afternoon—*this afternoon,* that changed. I figure if we just trim back your lines, cut one of your musical numbers, we'll be ready to open on schedule."

"Thanks, Mr. Sweeney," I said. "You can count on me."

¤

For the next few days my life fell into a routine organized around my role as Dylan Klebold. I woke early, went through my visualization exercises, only to find my father sitting silently on the bed beside me. Not even when I showed him my algebra homework, parabolas meticulously drawn across graph paper, could I persuade him to say anything. I had breakfast with my mother, who commented on the changes she saw in me. "I'm learning to use pain," I told her, "on account of the play."

After school I went to our dress rehearsals and worked especially hard on my monologue, even though Mr. Sweeney had cut it down to just seven lines. "You'll remember it better this way," he told me. I also worked with the choir director on my big number, "Making Pipe Bombs in Eric's Garage," until I could project my pain into the notes themselves—deep, heavy sounds, the music of distress. On stage, I felt I was becoming Klebold. I resented the students who played the victims for treating me so poorly. I disliked the students who played my teachers for not taking me aside, giving me a little pep talk and trying to point me in the right direction. I began to feel significant longing as well as a deep-seated resentment for Mike Rogers, who, as my only friend, Eric Harris, was clearly manipulating me into becoming his sidekick in the school shooting.

Everyone was impressed, even Robbie Fenstermaker, my predecessor, who occasionally attended rehearsals in a partial upper-body cast. Very carefully, he laid his good arm across my shoulders. "You're okay," he said. "You're not as much of a puss as I thought."

After the long weekend rehearsals, I felt the spirit of Klebold follow me outside the theater and into my regular life as a student. I intentionally spilled coffee on one page of my algebra homework. I showed up late to Social Studies two days in a row. In the gym, I mimicked noises of impatience when larger boys monopolized workout stations I wanted to use. On Wednesday, between classes, while focusing again on the incident with the dumbbells, I felt a regret open inside of me, a dark, soulful longing for a missing piece of my childhood. In that moment, I understood that this was how the rest of the world felt about their existence, this longing, this sorrow I had learned to manage through creative visualization techniques my mother learned about at the community college.

After rehearsal I always went home with Susan, who turned out to be my biggest fan. Virtually every afternoon, she asked me to recite my lines, to strut around like I was Klebold himself ready to storm into the school cafeteria. If I was feeling especially randy, I'd run through a piece of the "Manhattan Monologue" or list off two or three household items you could use to make a pipe bomb. As my reward, she'd strip off her clothes, garment by garment, until we were naked inside her mother's bed, having sex, then watching the Playboy Channel. By now I had a fair knowledge of the Playboy Channel. My favorite segments involved Mandy and Sandy, the Reinholt twins, demonstrating advanced Tai Chi movements in the nude.

On the night before our play opened, my mother confronted me about my behavior. "You've been walking around here like you own this place," she said. She crossed her arms, then uncrossed them. She was dressed in one of her shell pink suits. Shell pink was another recommended color for women in her field. "Your entire attitude has changed. I sense an anger coming from you, an anger I don't believe you're entirely in control of."

"It's not me, Mom. I'm practicing for the school play. I'm Dylan Klebold now. It's a big role. He carries a gun."

We walked to the living room couch and sat down. In recent years, I'd learned a great deal about life from her: how to handle anger, loss, a shrinking sense of yourself in the new world order. The trick to happiness, she'd once told me, was to realize you were no more important than anyone else. Our big mission in life was to get along peacefully with people different than us. In the tradition of these earlier lessons, that afternoon she told me, "You need to keep your emotions in check. We live in an age where we must put aside our own troubles so that everyone feels comfortable and safe." She placed her hand on my shoulder, a kind, disarming gesture I imagined was very effective with her clients at work. "You've been brooding around this house for over a week."

"I just want to be good in the school play," I said. "As good as Robbie Fenstermaker."

"You shouldn't hold yourself up to the standards set by others."

"But I do. I don't want everyone to think I'm a wuss."

"No one thinks you're a wuss. And if they do, you can tell yourself, Self, I'm not a wuss no matter what people think. That was your father's problem. He cared too much what other people thought and didn't know how to find the peace that was inside him all along."

That night I felt a strong discontent settle into my heart, the sense that I was living in a very small box—a comfortable box, furnished with a nice bed, nice bookshelves, a faux-antique lacquered desk where I did my homework, but a *small* box nonetheless. In my dream, I walked along a corridor lined with security cameras until I came to a white sand beach where I saw my father in his red Hawaiian shirt drinking a piña colada from a plastic cup. The sun slanted down onto my face, and in the distance, small waves curved ashore. "Don't be such an asshole," my father said to me. "Clearly Burma is the way to go." He was trying to hand a piña colada to me when I slipped away from the beach and into the darkness that marked the general landscape of my dreams.

In the morning, as I imagined my father sitting next to me on the bed, he was silent again, not the chummy, free-speaking individual I'd seen the night before. He didn't even look at me. When I walked in front of him, he offered me an expression of wide-eyed condolence before he patted his pockets in hopes of finding a new pack of smokes. In the shower, I practiced my two songs for the play, and when I returned, I found not only my father but the transparent image of Dylan Klebold sitting beside him on my bed. Klebold wore a black coat and sweater and had two bandoliers of ammo draped across his chest. He leveled me with his eyes, one of them discolored with a bruise. I could tell he was about to leave by the way his form kept growing lighter, but I asked him to stay, to tell me what I needed to know to be him on stage.

"Be me?" he laughed. "You have no idea how to be me. You drop a dumbbell on your foot. You think that's insight. You think that's pain. Ha. I wanted just one good friend. A friend to sit with me through the long, dark hours of the night. And when I find him, he turns out be a psycho-Nazi, intent on dragging my sorry ass down to the seventh level of hell. Go shove that in your school's piano and sing about it."

With that he was gone. My father gave me that sorrowful look once more before his body dissolved into the early morning light as well. I sat on the floor stunned. I felt empty, much like my mother must have felt when my father left, like someone had scraped my insides out with a stick.

In the gym, I waited for two football players to finish with the bench press. After five minutes I made my usual noises of impatience, but they pretended I wasn't there. One said, "You hear something?" The other responded, "Cut the comedy and throw on another ten pounds." In the breezeway I told a group of freshman to move away from my locker, only to have one respond, "Oh, bite me." In the cafeteria, I tried to push toward the fast window, only to have some girl elbow me in the spleen so hard I nearly doubled over.

Clearly I'd lost my connection to Klebold, that gossamer string that had tied our two hearts together for the past week. He'd appeared in my room just long enough to claim whatever part of him I'd found, then leave again. While sitting on the lawn with Susan, I did my absolute best to call up my Kleboldian self, to drag it up from the seventh level of hell and return it to its rightful place inside my chest. I recalled the exact details of the dumbbell falling on my foot, how I crumpled on to the neoprene mat so angry I could hit someone. I imagined the correct sound of Klebold's voice, the repressed edge of anger evident in it. When I was so focused I could almost hear it, I said, "Mother Fucker, this cheeseburger is a little cold."

Susan deadpanned me, her eyes entirely absent of lust. "Hey," she said, "are you coming down with something? You sound like you are. Maybe we shouldn't screw around today. I need to sound good tonight. I'm sending the video off with my Rutgers application." She scooped the remains of her lunch into a bag and slid away from me.

That afternoon at our final rehearsal we walked through each scene, practicing our lines and dance numbers, but saving our singing voices for the actual performance. I could tell Mr. Sweeney was disappointed in me because my voice wasn't right; neither were my gestures. I knew all my lines, but when I said them I sounded like "Library Victim Number Four," not Dylan Klebold. Mr. Sweeney didn't say anything, though. He kept glancing toward the theater seats, all of which were empty except for two. Reporters from the local *Sun-Times* sat quietly in the second row, yellow legal pads in their laps, expressions of guarded disbelief mapped across their faces. Mr. Sweeney couldn't have been more delighted. Between acts, while standing in the wings, I heard him tell Robbie, "You get attention any way you can."

At the intermission, he stepped to center stage and said what he usually did about our play, that it was a cautionary tale designed to expose real-world violence as the unacknowledged form of entertainment it had become. He was joined by Mr. Dickerson, vice president of the SafeCampus Corporation, who said how proud he was to sponsor a play with such vision, such enthusiasm for the high-tech, fully monitored world of the future. He told the reporters about the security retrofitting his company had already completed at our school. "With cameras like these in virtually every hallway, no crazed mutant is going to mow these kids down in an ambush. Ain't that right, kids?" We all said, "Yeah," as we'd been directed to do. He smiled while one of the reporters took his picture, the eight library victims arranged in a semicircle behind him.

All through my "Manhattan Monologue" I was nervous. I said my lines as best I could, while Mr. Sweeney projected his slides onto the white screen above me and the students who played the victims formed a row and pretended to hum the chorus of future dread, a number that had been significantly shortened so as to match the new length of my speech. Out of the corner of my eye, I could see Susan. She wore her striped sweater, her hands clasped behind her back. Like the other victims she pressed her lips together, though did not actually hum. How I wanted to impress her, to let her know we could find something in this play, some memory we could hold on to, a piece of our lives stitched together, but after rehearsal I didn't find her outside the girls' dressing room. Nor did I find her in Mr. Sweeney's office thumbing through those acting magazines she so liked to read.

I knew why she'd left. Of course I did. Because I wasn't the actor she'd hoped I'd be. During our one-hour evening break, I walked aimlessly around our school, past Officer Brubaker's security substation, past my clear plastic locker, past the half-completed kennel where our school planned to house a watchdog. I sat in the Humanities Courtyard beside a maple tree and asked Dylan Klebold to return to me. *I* will be your friend, I told him. *I* will listen to you through the long, dark hours of the night.

Across the courtyard, beneath a hand-painted banner the pep squad had posted for our football team, he appeared, translucent and fading, dressed in his black coat and sweater, his eye socket still bruised, his arms crossed. I walked slowly toward him, transfixed by the see-through iridescence of his face. He regarded me differently this time, his eyes wide, reconsidering. I saw he was a little like me, somewhat cautious, perhaps lonely, yet without anyone like Susan to help get him through those especially tough days.

I stopped a good ten feet from him because his form was growing dimmer. "What do you want?" he asked.

"To do a good job in the school play," I said, but he could tell I wanted other things as well.

"Experience doesn't come cheap."

"I know," I said. "I realize that." I started toward him again, his brown eyes fixed on me, an expression of pity falling across his face. He stood very still, arms at his side, not angry anymore, but sad for some reason. He vanished before I could reach him, leaving me alone with the security cameras and trash cans, early lines of moonlight washing the ground at my feet.

¤

By the time I returned to the drama wing, Susan was already in the girls' dressing room being fitted with blood packs. Outside the theater parents lined up, as did a few reviewers, most of them milling around an information booth staffed by representatives of the SafeCampus Corporation. I went to the boys' dressing room, where Mr. Sweeney handed me a black sweater very close in design to the one Klebold had worn in the Humanities Courtyard earlier that evening. He reminded me where my two weapons were kept, the TEC-DC9 and a shotgun with the stock and barrel sawed off, then handed me a clear plastic bag filled with carpenter's nails and another filled with bits of colored plastic made to look like broken glass. I was supposed to carry these props into "Eric's Garage" when I walked on stage for the first time.

Clearly he must have sensed how nervous I was, reviewing my lines, looking for Susan when I could. From behind the curtains, I saw my mother in the third row, her hands clasping a congratulatory Hall-mark card she had most likely signed earlier that day. Seeing her there, all pretty, waiting for my big performance, I felt bad all of a sudden because my father hadn't said a word to me all week, not even something as casual as "Break a leg, Kid," which was the type of thing he liked to say.

As the houselights dimmed, Mr. Dickerson took center stage. He introduced the play, repeating a number of things Mr. Sweeney had said that afternoon about violence and the role of musical theater, but concluded by saying, "Tonight's play has reminded me of the important service SafeCampus can offer to schools like yours all across the country."

As the curtains swung open, I can't tell you how nervous I was. I stood in the wings and watched the first act, the students who played the victims' parents sing "When Hitler's Birthday Comes to a Small Town Like Ours." Backstage, I looked for Susan. Twice I took small sips of water from our drinking fountain, even though Mr. Sweeney had warned us against this. Again I asked Klebold to return to me, to be with me tonight so I wouldn't be nervous, so I could say my lines as I had the week before.

While I waited for him to appear among the pulleys and ropes, I felt a hand on my shoulder—Mr. Sweeney's hand. How glad I was he was there with me, among the props constructed for "The Library" scene. He put his arm around me, just like I visualized my own father doing on those mornings when I had a big test or a student presentation. "You're getting nervous," he said, "aren't you?"

"A little," I confessed. "But I want to do a good job."

"I know you do." He guided me out of the shadows and toward the sound booth. From the music, I knew the time had almost arrived for me to step on stage, to claim the role as best I could. "Sometimes when I'm nervous," he said, "I picture something that motivates me. Like my name on an off-Broadway marquee. Nothing fancy, just small letters nicely fixed above the box office." He pulled me to his side, a very warm gesture, but as he did I saw Susan down the hall. We were at the exact right angle to see into the makeup room. She was examining herself in the mirror, her hair pulled into a ponytail, her face dusted with powder.

Beside her was Robbie Fenstermaker, his partial upper-body cast holding more student signatures than all three of my high school yearbooks combined. Then he did something odd, Robbie did; he slipped his good arm around Susan's waist very gently, so that she turned to him, her eyes wide and happy, just like they were in her mother's bedroom when she looked at me.

"Clearly," Mr. Sweeney continued, "you were the best choice for an understudy. I'm very glad you decided to take this role." He moved me toward the stage, but I kept glancing at the makeup room, my eyes darting around the other students in hopes that I might glimpse Susan again. As we waited in the wings, listening to Mike Rogers sing the song of teenaged hate, a feeling of rejection rushed into my heart, a feeling so strong I couldn't push it away no matter how hard I tried. In the audience, parents watched the stage intently. Around me students glanced my way with a certain callousness I'd never noticed before.

When the song changed keys, Mr. Sweeney handed me my bags of carpenter's nails and colored plastic. "You're the man," he said and gave me a little push. With the spotlight on me I walked across the stage, doing my best to move with determination and purpose; then I sat on a bench and pretended to empty Fourth of July fireworks into cylinders made of steel. When I started singing, my voice was louder than I expected, filled with a heartache so large Mike Rogers looked somewhat surprised to find this sound coming from me. I let this feeling swoop down around me, an arsenal of notes falling from my lips. I didn't care who heard: my mother, Susan, even Mr. Sweeney. I was doing my best, trying to remember what to say, where to stand, but in my mind, I was already at home, hoping Klebold would return so he could tell me what these feelings meant, where I should go from here.

Wrestling Al Gore

We had seen him as The Assassin, The Mongrel, and Diamond Eyes Malone, yet only when he became Al Gore did we notice the prophetic nervousness that shook his thin, freckled body. He appeared in a brilliant hoop of light, dressed in a blue wrestling singlet intended to look presidential, but for us—all of us, I believe—we were not reminded of Vice President Gore, but of the young Al Gore, the teenager who grew up a few miles from here, in Carthage, Tennessee. He carried only a single prop, a scuffed briefcase that he deposited on the announcer's table before taking his place in the ring.

Twice each year the WWL brought its wrestlers to our town. They rented the Ice Palace, covered its rink with plywood, and erected a raised ring identical to the one they used on their Sunday night TV show, *Power*. We'd grown up with wrestling. We'd seen the great Terry Funk defeat the Underlord. We'd been on hand as Andre the Giant pinned Mogar the Infidel using only a simple submission hold. Yet we'd never seen anything like this, a wrestler who so resembled one of our own, the local boy who ran for president—a guilty charge ran through us, a pulse of electricity, as we remembered how we'd let him down. We lived in a small state, responsible for only eleven electoral votes, yet we'd let those votes go to his opponent. We all believed we should have done something more.

Before the match the Ice Palace darkened so that our attention was drawn to the Sony JumboTron hovering like a window behind the ring. The screen lightened to the image of a news anchor standing before the White House, while the enthusiastic music of a military band marched in around us. Our spirits were briefly lifted by the tune, as well as by the crisp matter-of-fact manner with which the anchor summarized the election. The screen replayed news clips we knew so well: Gore asking for a recount, Kathleen Harris certifying the vote, judge after judge reversing a lower court's decision. "There are some people," the anchor concluded, "who believe Bush stole the presidency. Tonight the matter will be decided in the ring."

The wrestler who portrayed George W. Bush was a thin man with large arms and sandy hair. He wore black briefs with matching black wrist tape and shin pads that made him resemble the type of professional shootfighters we'd only seen on TV. His face bore dark shadows of recent bruises, and his nose was angled in such a way that we suspected it had been broken more than once. Surely we'd seen this wrestler before, his sleek Aryan form gracing the Ice Palace in years past, but we couldn't agree on his previous character. Some thought he'd been Thundar the Norseman, while others believed he'd been Mean Jack Sherman. We all believed he'd been a bad guy, a heel.

He paraded around the ring with two WWL Power Girls, pretending to be the champ, all the while looking to us, his audience, for support. When only a few people cheered, we heard the static of applause piped in through public address speakers. George W. Bush—or

"W," as the commentator called him—did his best to earn our respect. He made a show of raising his hands enthusiastically, a grandstanding maneuver. He pumped his arms so that his muscles contracted into impressive oiled knots. Before he lifted himself into the ring, a retired wrestler dressed in the robes of a Supreme Court justice presented him with an envelope clearly marked PRESIDENCY. W pushed it away before swinging his thick legs over the ropes, only to find Gore beside the referee, his lips twisted in a thin, ironic grin. It was the same Tennessee grin the real Gore had possessed as a boy.

The match began quietly, so unlike the other WWL matches we'd come to love. Neither wrestler made a speech, neither taunted his opponent. Silently they moved to the middle of the ring, trading forearm blows so realistically delivered we doubted their match had been choreographed. Early on we surmised that Gore was the better wrestler. He was broad-chested, quick with his hands. He knew how to cut a punch so we could hear its impact. He executed his kicks in such a way that the more knowledgeable members of our town suspected he'd studied Japanese wrestling tapes. How we followed him, his body forcing W to the ropes, the powertwist that brought his opponent to the mat in a failed attempt to pin him.

Each time Gore turned to us, we cheered—a long, low wail of a cheer. We sat in one section so the Ice Palace would appear full when videotaped. Gore seemed to be confused that we were pulling for him, a Democrat. When he fell to the mat, he seemed to be waiting for something, applause perhaps, as W rolled him into a leg hold. The markings of bewilderment passed across his face. His expression deepened to reflection, then resolve, before he kicked out and rose to his feet, his short black hair dripping with sweat.

How we wanted Gore to win—to pull W on his back and hold him there for the three count. Since the election we had not entertained such hope. We lived in a state with hills of layered stone, trees that offered their perfume all year round. We'd known the real Gore as a boy. We'd talked to him at Reed's Pharmacy and at the Ben Franklin. He was one of our own, a good boy—a man we'd let down.

In the ring he walked through the motions of exhaustion, favoring a loose uppercut because he was more skilled in fighting than in show wrestling. Twice he caught W in the chest, strong jabs that seemed to surprise them both, and once he performed a powerslam with such force that the two men slid dangerously close to the unpadded portion of a turnbuckle. But already we were beginning to sense how this match would end. We understood the drama of wrestling, the way a wrestler lost before he was pinned. There were clues: fatigue, illegal holds, condolence in a commentator's voice.

Still we cheered. We shouted his name. One of our children— Kevin Brockman's, I believe—yelled, "Open a can of whoop ass on him." Though Gore was doing his best to convince us he was spent, we sensed his actions were scripted. He moved awkwardly across the ring, pretending to be dazed. He favored a wild roundhouse that was telegraphed so clearly, W was able to step out of the way and hip-toss Gore into the ropes. We'd seen wrestlers go down in such carefully planned defeats many times, but we'd felt the justice of these previous decisions. They'd been simply a matter of good defeating evil.

Briefly Gore regained his strength, spinning out of a headlock. He delivered two high kicks, further convincing us of his Japanese training. Gaining speed off the ropes, he charged W. He lifted him across his shoulders, a fireman's carry so poorly delivered they both fell to the mat, where a newly energized W leapt to his feet, dropped a fast leg across Gore's chest, and held him for the full count, a classic finishing move.

The Ice Palace grew quiet, except for a few fans who were not from our town, as we watched the referee raise W's hand, the winner. There were other matches on that night's card, including a ladder match between Downtown Marvin Dark and a maniac who wrestled in a butcher's smock named The Cleaver. W and Gore departed the ring in silence. They did not engage in the customary post-fight interview, an arrangement that somehow made the defeat more devastating for us. We sat through the remaining matches somewhat subdued, not even rising when The Cleaver pulled a large kitchen knife from the lip of his boot.

In the days that followed we went about our lives much as we had for years. We were store owners, policemen, gas station attendants, repairmen. We continued to watch *Sunday Night Power* on TV, but did so mainly out of habit. For weeks, we lived with the hope that the Bush/Gore matches were evenly divided between wins and losses, but after Jason Sanders's cousin, Mitch, told us that Gore had lost in Jacksonville, we understood the scope of our problem was larger than we'd first suspected.

We all agreed that the WWL had a right to arrange their matches any way they liked. They were a business, after all. Yet we felt betrayed because they had not taken into account our feelings. We were lifelong fans. We'd purchased action figures for our kids. We loved the battle between good and evil. But how was this matchup an example of such drama?

Most people favored a town-wide WWL boycott, though I myself favored a more reasonable approach, a letter-writing campaign. Already the *Power* commentators were suggesting one of our favorite wrestlers, David "The Big Man" Brady, would fight in a title match later that year. I believed much good would come from all of us watching that match at Arnold Miller's house, seated in the folding metal chairs he kept in his basement. But before we arrived at a consensus, an interesting thing happened. *Parade* magazine published a short article about the Bush/Gore matchups.

The article, written by Barry Stein, explained that the matches, never televised, were something extra for the fans who showed up in person. He mistakenly compared the duel to previous political matchups, most notably The Iron Sheik's historic feud with Sergeant Slaughter. He described the bouts as "a realistic battle of brawn" and "an unlikely recount without the chads." He closed by quoting league CEO Lance Peterson's explanation: "Because WWL fans believe a decision as important as the American presidency should not rest in the hands of the Supreme Court."

We were quick with our reply, typing it that night with the help of George Houston, a junior high English teacher. We tried our best to be polite, but our indignity must have leaked into the letter as we pointed out important facts omitted in Mr. Stein's article, such as the exact manner by which wrestling stories developed into various good-versus-evil rivalries. As for the battle between The Iron Shriek and Sergeant Slaughter, Mr. Stein had neglected to mention that this rivalry unfolded in the late 1970s, while Iran was holding fifty-two American hostages. We wanted to conclude by demanding that *Parade* print a retraction, but at George Houston's suggestion we closed by stating that Gore's wrestling abilities far surpassed those of W and that there were many WWL fans who were disappointed to learn that Gore had been losing so many battles in the ring.

We posted the letter Monday morning by registered mail and expected to receive a call by the end of the week. I can't tell you how those days dragged by, all of us waiting for the phone to ring. But no such call came, nor did we receive a letter, not even a short one to acknowledge our concerns. All that month we checked *Parade* magazine, hoping to see a portion of our letter published in their editorial section, but instead they published readers' comments about Bob Hope and Spring Delight salad recipes.

I suppose our story might have ended there, with a shadow of skepticism darkening our town, but the following Tuesday Buddy Laneer brought us a WWL ad clipped from a Mobile paper, an ad that featured Gore and W standing toe-to-toe, fists raised like street fighters.

The caption read: "The Battle Continues." There was something about their pose, the clean white light angling onto Gore's face, that led us to believe the WWL had reconsidered its position on the two wrestlers' abilities.

We wrote our second letter that night at Denny's, all of us seated in the back booth reserved for large parties. We took a number of catchy phrases from our previous letter but were all in agreement that it had not gone far enough. In this version, we pointed out that Gore was more muscular, better trained, faster with his hands. His style was influenced by a Japanese tradition of wrestling that apparently W had never studied. We asserted that the WWL had misjudged its audience if they believed that a match so prejudicially scripted would satisfy loyal fans such as ourselves. We summarized the election results by stating: "although Al Gore lost the (questionable) electoral vote, he won the popular vote by over a million ballots." We closed by suggesting that the wrestling ring was a place where the injustices of the real world could be set right again.

We were pleased with the letter; each of its three paragraphs sounded strong and forceful. We read it out loud many times, all of us a little spacey on coffee, and Ken Carson, a man with some radio experience, suggested we change a word here and there so that we "sounded more hacked off." We gave the final draft to Ed Swift, who promised to type it by noon. As we were paying the bill, Ed suggested in an offhanded manner: "You know, we could send it anywhere the WWL has a show."

And so in this way we entered the political world of professional wrestling. Almost overnight we lost interest in other WWL matches, such as David "The Big Man" Brady's tag-team affairs, and focused our attention on Gore versus Bush. We started out slowly, mailing fresh copies of our letter to large-circulation papers in cities where the WWL had an upcoming show, but soon we were including color photographs of Gore and W so that anyone with two eyes could see that Gore possessed a strong physical advantage. We cited Gore's experience, listing his previous wrestling names, and revealing that to the best of our knowledge he'd won seventy-two percent of his matches. At the urging of Bunky McMahon, my neighbor, we began to include leftover campaign materials, such as bumper stickers and buttons, photographs that showed the real Gore as a good guy, one of our own.

Five times that month we saw our letter reprinted in papers such as the *Atlanta Constitution* and the *Miami Herald*. Almost always it was featured in the op-ed section alongside opinions about other important civic activities, but the *Orlando Sentinel* excerpted our letter in a short article entitled, "Familiar Controversy Enters the Ring."

On *Sunday Night Power*, we began to see Gore and W in the background. They didn't wrestle on TV but participated in the March of Champions and the singing of the national anthem. They stood reverently with the other wrestlers while the American flag was hoisted to the rafters. Many times we saw Gore talking to the fans, and once while he was chatting with the Texas Tag Team, Mitch Arnold, the voice of the WWL, said, "Look at the arms on that guy."

The first to learn about the Super Smackdown was Nick Sanders. According to an article in *Attitude*, the "mysterious Bush/Gore matchups would conclude in Knoxville." The article went on to quote liberally from an interview in which W hoped the matchups "would help the economy" and "let kids know the importance of a good education." In contrast, Gore offered very little except that to say, "Support of the presidency is important."

For the two months leading up to the Smackdown we sent packets to newspapers and magazines. We now included a brief biography of the real Gore's life as well as photos of his hometown. There was a nice shot of his childhood home and one of the small downtown shopping area. We included photos of the newly expanded Smith County High

School and of his family's farm. Though no one said as much, we felt that a rejection of Al Gore was a rejection of us. We suggested that if the American voting public could recast their votes, Gore might be in the White House right now.

We continued to watch *Power* in Arnold Miller's basement, in folding chairs arranged around his projection TV. For three weeks Gore and W were strangely absent from the show; then they reappeared in short "On the Road" segments. In the first such segment, we saw them in the ring, locked in a double cobra hold, an intensity in their expression we had not seen before. They appeared more bruised than we remembered. The segment also showed W dragging Gore to the ropes, but Gore was able to level two jujitsu kicks into W's ribs, thereby freeing himself.

This segment portrayed the wrestlers as evenly matched, but subsequent clips seemed to favor Gore, focusing on his devastating forearm jabs and powertwists. They depicted him as a rising underdog, a good guy, a man with an excellent physique. Two weeks before the Smackdown, he was allowed to briefly speak to the cameras: "There are some things I'd like to change in Washington," he said as a small line of blood trickled down from his eyebrow, "and my *Power* fans know just what they are."

We felt a variety of emotions: anticipation, doubt, confusion. We'd been misled by the WWL before other such pay-per-view events. But we all felt a turning in our chests, an unexpected fizz. We were men slightly beyond the peak of middle age. We had receding hairlines. We had trouble sleeping at night. We owned johnboats and American-made cars. We'd forgotten what it was like to want something this much.

In the days leading up to the Smackdown, reporters began to call us so as to better understand our position. We received calls from the *Tennessean* and *Smoky Mountain News,* but also from *Southern Living* and *Georgia Sports Weekly.* A reporter from the *Washington Post* at first thought our organization might be a joke, but we set him straight. The people in our town, we explained, were interested in preserving Gore's political popularity within the setting of the WWL ring. "We think he's the better man," we told him, "and the better wrestler."

In all we received seven requests for interviews, the most prominent appearing in the *Atlanta Constitution* on page D2, just below the fold. A number of our more important quotes were pulled from the text and enlarged in boxes. We explained that Gore had a good family name and that we didn't like to see his image so abused in public. Over the course of the article, the reporter gradually began to see the upcoming match for what it was: Gore defending his honor in Tennessee.

The Smackdown was held in the South Knoxville Sporting Center, home of the Riflemen, a much-loved indoor soccer team. Though we arrived early, we did not see any wrestlers milling around the WWL transport trailers. Nor did we see Mitch Arnold, voice of the WWL, interviewing fans for the pay-per-view home audience. We looked at souvenir T-shirts for such stars as The Leprechaun and Dave "The Big Man" Brady, all the while hearing stray bars of music that seemed suspiciously patriotic.

We felt the chemicals of nervousness move through our bodies, chemicals that were more powerful in the Sporting Center than they were at home. Though we did not talk about this, a few of us suspected that the Sporting Center had been designed to produce just this reaction—the jaundiced light, the ambient hum of the crowd, seats angled so we couldn't help but stare at the empty ring. We had come believing that other fans might recognize us, but such desires now seemed a childish vanity.

We did not see Gore during the March of Champions or during the national anthem. I don't think it would be an exaggeration to say the entire audience was disappointed. We all wanted to see him, this man who had grown up in our state. Had his muscles thickened?

Had he perfected the treacherous fireman's carry? We watched the first two matches patiently—tag-team bouts between youngsters—but kept scanning the backstage curtains, hoping to glimpse Gore's black hair, his blue wrestling singlet.

How the band teased us, launching into the CNN fanfare, offering a jazz riff of "Hail to the Chief" only to segue into the WWL theme music. When the Sony JumboTron brightened for the first time, we fell silent beneath its kaleidoscope swirl. Even the barkers stopped peddling their peanuts. But instead of the Recount preshow, we saw an ad for *Sunday Night Power*. They had us, these performers. They knew our hearts. We no longer gave a damn about The Leprechaun or even Mike "The Big Man" Brady. We only cared about Gore and to a lesser extent W.

At the start of the third match, we noticed a murmur move through the crowd, a whisper rolling like muted thunder. Bunky McMahon was the first among us to hear that a carload of wrestlers had been in an accident, a collision involving two vehicles. At first we believed this to be one of many WWL tricks we'd come to anticipate, the little ways the league tampered with our expectations, but then we noticed certain irregularities. Mitch Arnold interviewed wrestlers for an unusually long time, the technical crew cued up the same *Power* promo again, and then the clincher: the match between SpaceJack and Animal Morris was canceled.

Needless to say, we'd experienced other such cancellations, but there was something about this one, the way the announcers passed over it so quickly, that offered the confirmation we'd been dreading. Where was Gore? Was he at the Sporting Center at all?

Nervously we watched a ladder match between Jungle Jim and Awesome Dan Osborne but kept glancing toward the ominous backstage curtains. With the aid of Buddy Laneer's binoculars we attempted to read the teleprompter, but the words were too small. Jungle Jim and

Awesome Dan Osborne, sensing the crowd's lack of interest, began to step up their match, smacking each other with folding chairs, diving from the apron, elbow first. They moved into the stands, exchanging jabs, and then continued out to the concessions area, followed by remote cameramen.

We'd seen many such fights on pay-per-view, most working their way through the parking lot, mimicking the action of street brawls. But before the wrestlers returned to the Sporting Center, the houselights dimmed as an unsettling progression of minor chords swelled through the darkened arena. We saw two silhouettes emerge from the curtains. Before we could make positive identification, the Sony JumboTron blossomed into the image of an American flag rippling in the wind, accompanied by the voice of a news anchor: "Tonight the matter will be decided in the ring."

The crowd began to drum its feet, flashbulbs bathed the arena. In their strobe we could almost make out the two wrestlers, their sleek presidential forms, their neatly clipped hair. W appeared first in the harsh light of an unfiltered spot, wearing his trademark black wrist tape and shin pads. He motioned toward the crowd with less confidence than he'd exhibited at the Ice Palace. He didn't engage in such grandstanding gestures as raising his arms or holding up a single finger to indicate victory. Instead he stood stiffly beside the ring as the crowd noise softened to a buzz.

As the light encompassed Gore, fans rose, stomping their feet in a rhythmic march. We were Gore fans for the most part, though some members of the audience, I must admit, seemed to favor W. How we wondered at him, his thick wrestler's arms, his sculpted legs. He appeared taller and more confident than he had at the Ice Palace, and for these reasons, he no longer reminded us of the young Gore but of the older one, the presidential candidate.

We admired him for a full ten or fifteen seconds before we noticed the purple line of a subcutaneous bruise half hidden by his wrestling singlet. We noticed it as a group, this dark band of skin slick with ointment, and we stopped cheering. Silently we watched him move toward this ring. Clearly he favored his right leg. Though he was doing his best to pretend he wasn't injured, we could see these simple movements required effort.

Mitch Arnold met him at the ring and did something we'd never seen him do before: he talked to a wrestler privately without his microphone, his arm draped avuncularly across Gore's shoulders. We understood, each of us, what was happening. A match as important as this was between the wrestlers and the fans: no interviews, no commentary.

We suspected Mitch Arnold was asking Gore to reconsider—Did he feel up to it? How bad were his injuries?—but Gore waved him away. He progressed into a series of stretches, limbering his arms and back. Only then could we see the extent of the bruise, a deep line cut diagonally across his chest, and a smaller one on his shoulder, an ink blot, a mark we'd later claim looked strangely like a face. But on that night we were only aware of his pain, how the beautiful mechanism of his body was broken in ways we would never understand. We shouted his name. We held up signs that said, "Gore Kicks Ass." He looked at us, his dark eyes seeming to understand that we'd worked to bring him here. We believed in him in ways we'd failed to believe in the real Gore. As he climbed into the ring, the Sporting Center erupted into cheers, women yelling at the top of their lungs, men cupping their hands so he might hear exactly what they had to say.

Of course we'd seen wrestlers perform while injured—most notably Slim Sanders with three fractured ribs—but we'd never seen an injured wrestler move as gracefully as Gore. The match began slowly, the two wrestlers circling each other, exchanging forearm blows. Gore did his best to protect his chest, covering it with his left arm. In W's defense, I must point out that he did not take advantage of Gore's injuries. He connected with his good shoulder, his stomach. He executed two Russian leg sweeps, presumably to end the match early, but Gore was strong.

Despite his injuries he was able to push W against the ropes and roll him onto the mat. In such moments we were intensely aware that these men were better trained in the true art of wrestling than they were in the flashy entertainment wrestling we were accustomed to viewing on TV. We were stunned at the classical holds they employed: leg holds, arm grips, snake ties. But they were WWL wrestlers as well. Because his upper body was injured, Gore favored his legs, delivering a number of short martial arts kicks to W's ribs. Twice W attempted to bodyslam Gore onto the mat and, missing, leapt to his feet, poised to deliver a midbody suplex.

Oh, how we ached for Gore each time he fell onto his wounded shoulder, each time his body was draped over the ropes, but he recovered, limping and dazed, moving in such a way that his pain seared us, too. He walked with a limp and held his left wrist as though it, too, was now injured. He absorbed a number of blows. He was good at taking bumps. We could see that he was tired, yet he stayed with us. He attempted to dropkick W to the mat. He pulled off a surprise lariat. He had stamina, this man. We believed the entire crowd was pulling for him, even those who'd earlier favored W.

While the two men were against the ropes exchanging tight blows, Jungle Jim and Awesome Dan Osborne returned to the arena, tired and muddy, having finished their parking-lot brawl. We saw complex emotions pass over their faces: pity, concern, an exaggerated sense of injustice. They approached the ring, towels draped across their shoulders, and stretched their hands, tag-team-style, toward Gore. Even though Gore was bleeding—he'd cut his eyebrow—he would not tag in a replacement. By waving his arm, he indicated he was not interested in their offer, yet Jungle Jim and Awesome Dan Osborne remained leaning into the ring, wondering at the raw courage and stamina Gore possessed.

We had not seen anything like this in years. How could Gore take it? He received blow after blow, sidestepping those he could, attempting to pull W onto the mat when he had the chance. Clearly he was tired. Was he wearing his opponent down with purpose? We were on our feet, yelling encouragement. Briefly Gore looked our way, a line of blood gracing his temple. In that moment we understood he was wrestling for us—all of us who believed in him.

I can't tell you how much we admired him just then. Did we admire him more than the real Gore? We weren't sure but felt a surge of guilt as we contemplated that possibility. We'd come here to save Gore. But with each forearm jab, with each splendid kick, he was saving us, letting us know that we were important, that our efforts had mattered.

He attacked with a beautiful combination of high punches. He executed a sweeping kick so stunningly performed that we momentarily forgot he was injured. But he had trouble maintaining his position. He seemed unable to straighten his left knee. Once he grabbed his sides— was he cramping?—but quickly recovered into a more protective stance. Many times he turned to us, his fans, arranged in the arc of the bleachers, his eyes glazed with a confident sheen as though he could see the towns where we lived, our brick houses, our front porches lined with chairs.

Gore did his best to pin W. Twice he charged him with a lowered shoulder. Once he grounded him with a Roman arm hold. But he was using the ropes for support. He let himself be backed into a corner. In a move some newspapers would describe as "merciful," W pulled Gore into a forward roll, a surprisingly sophisticated maneuver, followed by a shoulder pin. They were on the mat, W moving in for the close. We were quiet as we watched, so quiet we could hear the unmiked referee issue the full count.

We remained silent, unsure what we should do now that Gore had lost. We felt a strong reverence, yet we felt relieved as well. A man in the front row began clapping, his hands high above his head; then we were all clapping, the sound building like the roar of a well-tuned engine. We understood that this was what wrestling was all about, this tumble of emotion, this chill. Gore rose to regard us with his swollen fighter's face. He was a loser yet again. But he was *our* loser, the greatest loser who ever lived.

Arise and Walk, Christopher Reeve

I first heard the news from William, gardener for the Reeve family, as we sat on my back porch drinking port wine from the small glasses my wife Edna liked to save for orange juice. William was a tall, thin man, his hair as black as mine was gray, and was in the custom of wearing overalls even during the warm summer months. He was a little drunk, as was I, and had a toothpick set in the corner of his mouth. We sat, quietly watching the moon hover like an ornament above the Collinses' wooden gazebo, when he turned to me, his expression set in such a way I knew he wanted to convey information of some importance. "They're going to do it," he told me, "those doctors. He talked them into it."

"What are you talking about?" I asked.

"Mr. Reeve," he explained, removing the toothpick. "All that stuff with the lab rats, it's true. How they can fix up the spine. They're going to try it on humans, and he's the first." He leaned toward me conspiratorially. "You can't go telling anyone else, but I thought Edna would want to know."

"Edna? Edna's the last person I'd tell. You're just drunk, Will."

"Say what you like, but you understand what I'm talking about."

It was true. I did.

I was not a particularly well-educated man. I'd been brought up in an age when boys either prepared for college or for a trade. I'd trained to be gardener and caretaker. I'd learned the basics of plumbing and woodworking, as well as how to cultivate the plants that grow in this part of the country. But over the past few years I'd taken an interest in current events. I wanted to know things about this world before I left it. I followed *Time* magazine and read the newspaper each night. So I understood what William had told me, that our neighbor and William's employer, Mr. Reeve, might receive some special treatment with cells that could help mend his body. Stem cells, I believe. It was illegal to use these in our country, and because of this I thought William had got his facts turned around. "You go on, Will," I told him. "You're just trying to stir up gossip. No one loves a good tale as much as you."

"Honestly. I thought Edna would want to know. Otherwise why would I tell you in the first place?"

I offered him a look, then divided what remained of the port between our glasses. He changed the topic to pruning but appeared visibly disappointed I hadn't indulged his story. He left quietly that night, walking up an Italian flagstone path I'd laid ten years ago, before continuing onto the moonlit road that would take him to a similar cottage he occupied down the hill.

I stayed on the back steps for a long time, enjoying the quiet. I looked at the Collinses' house, a house I'd helped maintain for some thirty years, and beyond it to the Reeves' estate. Mr. Reeve owned a traditional Berkshire home centered on a large parcel of land, a long white house with an octagonal bedroom at one end, a living area at the other.

He also owned a barn, which once housed three horses but was now empty except for William's gardening tools. For many years, Edna had taken pride in living so close to a man as famous as Mr. Reeve. She'd followed his movies and kept track of his comings and goings. But all that ended a few years ago.

Around midnight I retired to my cottage, finding it dark except for the kitchen. I proceeded to do what I did each Sunday. I counted out the week's pills into daily boxes. I gave us each a multivitamin and a small red pill for blood pressure, but Edna also received white hormone tablets and blue caplets for her memory. We both understood what these blue caplets meant. They were designed to put off inevitable loss, but following her lead, I'd stopped talking about them some months ago. I found Edna as I'd left her in bed, her hair a graceful veil, her face untroubled, her hands gently turned around the satin edge of the blanket. I watched the expansion of her chest, the small motions of her lips and jaw. We were different people now that we were old. She stayed in the cottage, cooking and staring out the kitchen window. She'd let her friendships fall away and was no longer interested in crossword puzzles or afternoon games of gin rummy. Her only hobby was writing, filling up a small book with her own memories so that I might read them back to her some day. Dressed in my flannel pajamas, I lay beside her, our bodies close under the sheet, my arm hooked around her waist. I fell asleep wishing what I often wished, that our lives would open again, even if that opening lasted only a short while.

¤

The following day I woke later than I'd planned, at half past seven, and found Edna at our kitchen table dressed in a flannel bathrobe, her hair pulled back with a wooden clip. She looked so pretty in the morning sun, so serious as she leaned over her journal. Only when I kissed her neck, touching my lips to her skin, did she grudgingly acknowledge my presence. "So you've fallen into drinking with Will and rising when you feel like it?"

"I'm considering a career as a barfly. I've always wondered what goes on at AA meetings."

She handed me her coffee cup so I could refill it at the stove. "You wouldn't like AA. It's all about regrets and lost opportunities."

"I could talk about that," I said.

"What opportunities have you lost?"

"School," I said, taking a seat opposite her. I poured milk into my cup and nudged the sugar toward her. "I regret not taking an interest in school when I was young, not learning more about history and the like."

"You're doing that now." She said these things in a breezy, playful voice, so I'd understand she was teasing, then handed me the morning paper. "Why don't you sit here a while?" she said.

Even though October had only recently arrived, the morning was cold, the hills blanketed with crisp, Canadian air, blades of grass whitened with a slushy frost. I went about my Monday chores, giving the potted plants a good drink, blowing leaves from the back lawn. Many years ago I'd spent Mondays cleaning up after weekend parties—parties organized by professional caterers—but now that only Mrs. Collins remained in the big house my duties were simple enough: maintain the yard, clean the window screens, replace the outdoor lights, keep the walkways swept, the birdbath full.

When I was young I'd liked my job because I was good at it. Mr. Collins had appreciated my organization and attention to detail. But now I liked my job because it gave me time to think. Often I considered things I'd read in the paper. I'd come to understand many things about politics and even finance. But on that particular morning I thought about my own life, namely how few regrets I had. True, I'd wanted children at one point, but aside from that, I could think of no other regrets of substance, other than the one that was developing just then. I wanted to take this disease from Edna. I wanted her to feel young again. I wanted us to be in love, to spend hours playing cards or walking through the foothills.

We didn't refer to her disease by name, but it was there with us, in the way she occasionally forgot a word or paused mid-sentence. Little things, such as the inability to recall a book she'd read, sent her into an afternoon's depression. She was afraid of the worst, that she would gradually forget the important details of her life, the most recent memories falling away first, until she could no longer navigate the maze of her past, unable to recognize even her own reflection in a mirror. I had trouble picturing her this way because she was so bright and such a good reader, but my reassurances early on had only caused her to worry all the more.

As I rested on the side lawn, my gloved hands folded over a rake handle, I noticed activity at the Reeves' estate, two white vans parked in the driveway. The Reeves lived a short way from us, just down the hill, on land that had been a farm pasture when I first moved to the region. I supposed they'd been there all morning, those vans, with their back doors swung open, only I hadn't noticed them. They were long, sleek vehicles with tinted glass and AC units attached to their roofs. I watched as a woman dressed in blue scrubs—a nurse perhaps—carried not one but two IV stands up Mr. Reeve's front steps. I wouldn't have thought much of it—so many medical people visited Mr. Reeve's house—except for what William had told me the night before.

I waited quietly, watching. I noticed how nicely William had trimmed the Norwegian elms, how he'd worked junipers around the lawn where Mr. Reeve's son practiced soccer. I noticed, too, the way their barn was fading, a transparent salmon, in need of a fresh coat of paint. I hoped to see someone else exit the van. Its interior light was still on, but no one did. I scanned the Reeves' yard, but it, too, was silent.

Where was William today? I would have stayed there longer, except Edna called me to lunch. Only then did I realize how long I'd been staring across the road—a good fifteen minutes. I set my rake against the house, folded my gloves, then walked the short distance home.

As I ate I noticed that Edna was nervous. She stood at the sink, chopping celery on a large, wooden board, small tremors running through her hands. The light mood so evident this morning was gone, replaced by dim anxiety. When she didn't sit at the table, I joined her at the sink, taking the knife from her hand. "It's too early to start with dinner," I told her.

We stood there, two people married all these years, yet in moments like this I didn't understand her. I could only make an educated guess at her mood and disposition.

"Why don't you come sit with me?" I suggested.

"I don't mind fixing dinner. It makes me feel useful."

"What's this all about? You were happy this morning."

"It's nothing."

"It's not *nothing*."

She nodded, a gesture that directed me to her journal, laid face-down beside bowls set out to dry. I opened it carefully as I had a few times before, finding each page filled with her meticulous copperplate. Her writing was so beautiful that she could have easily become a secretary or a personal assistant. Her most recent entry was bookmarked with an envelope. She'd written about the day we first moved into our cottage, the mess she'd found here, the holes in the kitchen floor.

She looked at me pleasantly as I read, so I continued through the entire entry, which only filled up half a page. She was able to include many details, such as the original color of the bedroom walls (a darkly stained cherry) and the way our parlor, those early years, often smelled of lemon basil that grew wild near our back porch. I was surprised that the entry was so short because she tried to write a couple of pages each day. I complimented her on the fullness of her memory, how she could remember things I'd long forgotten, but my compliment was lost on her.

"Turn back five pages," she instructed.

On that page, I found her entry from two days before, the ink a slightly lighter shade of blue. She'd filled two whole pages with her lovely, slanted writing. After only a few sentences, I understood. This entry was nearly identical to the one she'd started this morning, a clear description of our cottage some thirty years ago. She'd described the bedroom walls with the same words, then continued to write about the fragrance of basil. This entry, though, talked of other things—our efforts to replace the bathroom sink as well as the night we papered the kitchen shelves.

"I don't remember writing that," she told me. "I wrote half my entry this morning, when I happened to flip back and found I'd written the same thing two days ago." She crossed her arms, then uncrossed them in frustration. "I was told it would happen this way."

I took her in my arms, even though she resisted, and clasped my hands behind her back. "That doesn't mean anything," I told her.

She stood quietly, her body stiff as wood.

"Half the time I can't remember where I left my tools."

"It's not the same," she said.

But I didn't say anything because she was right. I might lose my memory in small, average ways. As I held her, I began to understand her current range of fear, how brave she must be, able to take in with a full mind all those things she might some day lose.

I delayed my return to work by a full hour. I put away the vegetables she'd been cutting and sat beside her while she read one of her novels. I shuffled a deck of cards—not too long ago she'd loved playing cards after lunch—but she shook her head, refusing my offer. So I sat with her, our shoulders touching, and looked through the day's mail. Ads mostly. No bills. Not even *Time* magazine.

For the rest of the afternoon I stayed close to the cottage, cutting and edging the large front lawn. When Edna left for the farmers' market I asked if she wanted company. She waved me off in such a way a stranger would think I was crazy to ask.

"You still planning to join AA?" she said in a practiced voice, an attempt to be the person she'd been this morning, though I noticed her eyes held a sheen from crying.

I hooked an arm around her. "Don't think they'd take me," I said and kissed her on the brow.

She walked slowly down our road, off toward the market. Only after she'd disappeared did I allow my gaze to shift to the Reeves' estate. The house was dark except for the large, octagonal bedroom. The driveway held only one van.

✗

The following day I woke with the sun. I found Edna in our kitchen, writing in her journal as she did most mornings. I refilled her cup while I waited for my toast. I could tell she was feeling better simply by the way she looked. Her eyes were clear, her lips turned up in a thin smile. She pretended not to notice me trying to read over her shoulder. I checked her pill box to make sure she'd taken her pills, which she had, then took mine with some juice.

I expected to have a quiet morning, but when I sat beside her, she turned my way, her expression giving way to a lightness I hadn't seen for weeks. She looked younger, though perhaps it was an effect of the light. "What's happened to Will?" she asked.

"I haven't seen him since Sunday. Perhaps he's with his sister—down south."

"It's not like him to leave without telling you."

"Why all this interest in Will?"

"Just making conversation," she said.

I spent the morning repairing sprinklers, but every hour or so I walked to the edge of the property so I might see Mr. Reeve's house. I would have thought Mr. Reeve was not home—the house was that quiet—except for the gray sedan his morning nurse, Mrs. Rice, had parked out front. From talking with William I knew Mr. Reeve woke before dawn. Mrs. Rice dressed him and exercised his limbs so they wouldn't become stiff. She assisted him in and out of the new wheelchair he'd purchased the year before. Standing there, I watched for movement behind curtains, but the house was still, the porch empty.

I was about to go to lunch when a Mercedes eased up our street and stopped beside Mr. Reeve's barn. From the backseat emerged two gentlemen carrying large, leather satchels. Mrs. Reeve met them at the door, that is, the second Mrs. Reeve. She was a young, pretty woman, thin and with short dark hair. Even from this distance, I could detect her seriousness, the way she looked at the men, how she kept putting her hands into her pockets then taking them out.

Returning for lunch I found Edna on the front porch. She wasn't writing or even reading one of those novels she so liked. Rather she was looking off toward the yard, these two acres I'd worked for over half my life. The yard was not what it had once been, with large, seasonal gardens, but it was still a handsome yard—nicely groomed with touches of color here and there. I thought she might be remembering our years here, but as I drew close, I saw she wasn't looking at the Collinses' yard at all. She was looking down the road, her gaze settled on the Reeves' estate. I noticed other people—local farmhands—walking past the thick stone wall, peering from time to time toward Mr. Reeve's house as well.

For lunch that day, Edna reheated the white bean soup she'd made over the weekend. We fell into our usual routine: she stood at the stove while I sliced bread and set butter on a plate. Yet she appeared different that day—stronger, more comfortable with herself, pleasantly determined.

We didn't eat at the table but in the living room, as had been our custom years ago. I began to read *Time,* an article on the Middle East, yet I kept glancing at Edna. She sat with her legs tucked under her, much in the manner of a younger woman. Eventually we fell into conversation. She told me she was going take the car to town, that she wanted to buy some books and a new dress. She had not been to town in months, so I thought it an excellent idea. After we cleared away our dishes, I shuffled a deck of cards, expecting to be dismissed.

To my surprise she reached for a pad and pencil. "OK," she said reluctantly.

We hadn't played in months, not since she'd become worried over her memory, but now we were slipping back into those people: she contentedly retired, me working two-thirds time. Many years ago she'd worked for the Collinses, arranging special events. After Mr. Collins died, she'd found work at the five-and-dime. Not so long ago she'd known many people in town, other people like her who'd held domestic positions. She'd had a nice circle of friends, most of whom played hearts twice a week, but since winter she'd let these friendships fall away. She lost herself in books and magazines. She began writing a life journal, two pages a day, and labeled family photos so she would remember the events in them. We played three hands, that is, until she accumulated enough points to win.

Walking to the front porch, I felt an ease come over me, a satisfaction I remembered from the early days of our marriage. I liked being married to her and didn't know how I'd get on in the world without her. I walked to our driveway, my work gloves tucked under my arm, and opened the car door for her. She kissed me on the cheek. I watched the car move down the street, slowing as it passed the Reeves' estate, then continuing toward the highway that would take her to town.

¤

We didn't talk about Mr. Reeve, but that knowledge was there between us. For the rest of the week we took late breakfasts on the front porch, a pot of coffee set on a TV tray, both of us bundled in flannel shirts and thin wool gloves, the morning paper left unread at my feet. We pretended not to look at the Reeves' estate, but of course we did. We were aware of every car passing through his gates. We knew the regulars— nurses on rotating shifts, various aides, Mrs. Reeve's personal friends— but there were cars we hadn't seen before, some with tinted windows, a van with a satellite dish attached to its roof. Edna never mentioned these except to say, "Everything's so busy this time of year."

During the workday I took breaks so I might walk to the side yard. More than once I saw small groups of local residents, three or four perhaps, stop at Mr. Reeve's estate and peer through the decorative iron gate. The house stayed dark, the curtains pulled, but in the yard I noticed William at work again. Namely I saw that the rose bushes had been pruned and that the herb garden had been covered with a makeshift plastic tent for winter.

At lunch Edna was usually in a good mood, wearing nicely pressed clothes I hadn't seen in almost a year. She played cards, and more often than not she won. She wrote in her journal each day, but I saw evidence of other activities: articles clipped from magazines, a book on new treatments for her disease. On some of these articles she'd written notes, commenting on pills available in France, gene therapy being tested in Germany. She underlined a passage from a *Times* editorial stating: "the FDA is too cautious to approve treatments available elsewhere." Still she was reluctant to discuss these things with me.

Despite this I was happy to be with her. From our thirty years together, I knew she liked to think about a problem by herself. When we were young, trying to start a family, she hadn't told me about her doctor's report—that because of ovarian cysts the odds were against us—until she'd considered the matter at length. So I believed we'd entered a similar period, one where she needed to explore her possibilities in private.

On the following Monday, when I found her staring blankly out the kitchen window, I stood beside her, believing something in the yard had captured her attention, but the lawn was empty, the sky gray with clouds. She seemed to not even recognize my presence. Only when I put my arm around her did she finally notice me. It was a gradual recognition, as if she were in the dark basement of her soul and having trouble climbing the steps that led back to her body.

I expected her to be upset, as she had been after previous episodes like this, but instead she quietly went outside, a glass of water in her hand, and sat on the porch. We stared off at the Reeves' estate almost out of habit, her hand holding mine in such a firm, close manner I understood that she was happy I was with her just then, that she loved me in ways I might never fully know. With noticeable effort she began to talk—about little things really, that she'd phoned two of her old friends, that she was considering taking a part-time job again. When she felt better, she asked me to walk with her.

We walked through a small park, past a building that had once been a nursery school, along the fence of the Bodies' estate, presently unoccupied and listed for sale. We talked about events we remembered, parties we'd helped arrange, the time President Carter vacationed down the road. In certain ways, I felt the muted enthusiasm of youth enter me. Though I have never stopped loving Edna, I felt my love more pointedly on that night than I had on any in the past year.

She stopped at Mr. Reeve's estate, the last before we returned to our cottage, and ringed her hands around the thick iron bars of his security gate. We were just like those other curious people. But then I noticed Edna's expression change, turn serious and contemplative, as though her connection to Mr. Reeve was somehow larger than it had been during those years when she followed his career as a fan. She touched my arm, asking me to spy on these people we liked to think of as our neighbors. Though I'd spent the better part of the week observing this house from a distance, I felt uneasy turning my gaze upon it now. To my surprise I was able to see into the master bedroom, a view blurred by diaphanous curtains, yet I could make out the indisputable shape of Mr. Reeve seated in his special chair while a nurse—the evening nurse, Mrs. Dickerson, I believe—removed a thick bandage from the base of his neck and dabbed at that area with what appeared to be a sponge.

We stood quietly, both of us understanding what we'd seen, the aftercare following an operation, one much less invasive than I'd imagined. We stayed until Mr. Reeve was wheeled to a different part of the house. Before we continued home, Edna squeezed my arm. In a voice slightly deeper than was natural to her, she whispered, "It's amazing what doctors are able to do now." From that one sentence, I understood her fascination: she believed the medical miracles administered to Mr. Reeve might also save her mind from the disease growing ever so slowly within it.

¤

Following this, Mr. Reeve entered our lives in a new way. We didn't talk about his operation directly at first. Rather, Edna would comment on a car she'd observed at his house, or I might tell her about a Federal Express package I saw delivered. But after a day or two she began to speculate about his condition. "I wonder if he'll walk," she mused, "or if he'll be able to drive a car."

She became more lighthearted, more interested in life around our cottage. She filled our birdfeeder with seed and tied back curtains so our dining room was filled with sunlight again. Yet I watched these improvements with relative unease. She'd never been one to hope for miracles. Even when she'd learned about her ovarian cysts, she'd accepted the prognosis gracefully. We hadn't sought the help of fertility specialists. Instead we'd resigned ourselves to fate. If we weren't meant to have children then we wouldn't have them. But now, faced with what she might lose, she pictured herself as the beneficiary of medical advances, orchestrated in part, it seemed, by our neighbor down the street.

We continued to take our breakfast on the porch, the coffee between us, the mid-fall sun low on the horizon. By now I understood what Edna was doing. She was struggling to become the person she'd been some years ago, more at ease and comfortable. The two times she stopped mid-sentence, words suddenly lost to her, she didn't allow depression to overcome her, nor did she wonder if her disease might be advancing faster than the doctors had predicted. She simply worked her way back into language. She forced herself to keep talking—about the yard, about books, about memories she was recording in her journal.

In truth I wanted nothing more than to help her become this person. Though I never told her as much, I began to stay around the cottage, making up little jobs in the Collinses' large front yard. I trimmed back a decrepit maple tree; I assembled a wooden bench Mrs. Collins had wanted me to assemble for weeks; I straightened the shale border that separated her yard from her neighbor's.

From time to time, Edna came to the front porch, often to write in her journal or to read. She was good at spending long hours by herself, but over the past day or two, I'd noticed a restlessness in her, a shifting of sorts. When I returned for lunch that Tuesday, I found her seated by our phone, a fancy cordless model Mrs. Collins had given us for Christmas. She appeared so lost I immediately assumed she was experiencing a momentary absence, yet when I touched her arm, she turned to me, wide-eyed and confident. "I'm thinking about calling my friends," she said.

"Why don't you?"

"I haven't called them for so long I imagine they're mad at me."

"That's ridiculous," I told her.

Instead of picking up the phone, she moved beside me, her fingers gently circled around my arm. "Maybe after lunch," she said.

I was about to tell her she was only putting off something that would make her happy, when I heard a knock at our door. It was William, dressed in his overalls, mud on his knees, work gloves tucked into a pocket. He asked to borrow a post-hole digger, but we both knew why he was here. "A digger?" Edna said. "You aren't going to start putting in posts right before lunch, are you?"

I got out three plates while William told us about his trip to his sister's. I glanced at Edna only once—she leaned against the stove—noting her pleasure at William's arrival. "It's like, I'm supposed to think my vacation was some big gift," he said, "but they're not fooling anyone. I'm surprised the tabloids haven't shown up yet."

"No one wants the tabloids to show up," Edna offered.

"But why do they have to keep everything a secret? Who am I going to tell?"

"You've told me," I told him.

"Other than you. I mean, I'm like a lawyer with one of those confidentiality agreements. It's those aides you have to worry about. You can't buy loyalty for nine dollars an hour. Without them, I wouldn't know anything myself."

Over lunch William told us more about his trip and his plans to move near his sister someday. Just as we were finishing, I saw something I hadn't seen in two weeks: Mrs. Reeve wheeled her husband onto their front porch. I was the first to see him there, wearing a gray sweater, an afghan covering his legs. They sat side by side looking out at their yard, much like Edna and I liked to do. Noticing my silence, William followed my gaze, as did Edna. We were quiet neighborhood voyeurs, all of us too interested to talk.

After a few minutes Mrs. Reeve did something curious. She took her husband's arm and unfolded it, much like a bird's wing, then folded it back. She did this four or five times before Edna said, "She's exercising his muscles." I saw that this was true. She was giving his arms a good stretch, yet after she had finished her regime, her husband's arms lay at his sides, useless as wood.

"That's the sad thing," William said. "She's been doing that all week. They sit in the back for hours while she moves his arms one at a time." He looked at his hands, then placed them in his lap. "It's to stimulate *independent* muscle movement. The doctors thought he'd be able to move his arms by now. You know, in little ways."

"Already?"

"From what I hear, if he doesn't move his arms soon, they'll know the treatment isn't working."

"How soon is soon?" Edna asked.

"Next day or two, I imagine." He offered us an odd expression, one I could only read as a condolence. "It doesn't need to be much," he added, "only a little movement—a start."

After lunch I found the post-hole digger for William, and when he was gone I returned to find Edna on our front porch, a cup of coffee in her hand. She faced the Reeves' estate, though by now their porch was empty. When I touched her arm, she seemed surprised to find me there, but then appeared herself again.

We returned to the cottage and washed dishes as we did most days after lunch, Edna at the sink, me with the towel. I could tell she was struggling to keep an easy mood, a struggle that made me like her a great deal. When she said, "I admire him," it was as though we'd been talking about Mr. Reeve the whole time.

"Me, too."

"I want him to raise his arms. I want him to walk."

I placed my hand on her shoulder. She was trembling, close to tears. "I want him to walk," she repeated.

I didn't say anything, but let those words float in the room with us, burnish us with their naked hope.

That afternoon I mowed the back lawn and skimmed leaves out of the fish pond Mrs. Collins kept because her grandchildren enjoyed it. Still, I found excuses to wander to the side yard. The first two times I saw only Mr. Reeve's large house, the octagonal bedroom lit from inside, his yard empty except for William, who was fixing a riding mower. On my third trip, I saw Mr. Reeve sitting on his porch while his son practiced soccer. He still wore a gray sweater, his hands folded in his lap. I paid close attention to his movements, the way he turned his head, even how he shrugged his shoulders. All the people in the neighborhood knew Mr. Reeve could move his head, even his shoulders some, but his arms were lost to him, as was the rest of his body. How I wanted to see those arms move, rise even an inch under his own power, but he sat quietly, watching his son with a great earnestness. When the afternoon light began to drain from the sky, Mr. Reeve maneuvered his chair down a long wooden ramp. He was able to direct its movements through a straw he put in his mouth—he blew into it, I suppose—and when he was parked at the edge of the grass he continued to watch his son, offering words of encouragement. When the ball stopped within inches of his feet, he was able only to watch as his son walked over to retrieve it.

I was moved by Mr. Reeve's tender expression. A few cars passed, as did two people on foot, all of whom looked toward his house. I returned to our cottage early that day, expecting to find Edna disheartened, but she hadn't seen Mr. Reeve. She sat on our sofa, a book open in her lap, *Strategies in Popular Card Games.* It was a book she'd flipped through many times. "I called Shirley and Elizabeth. Linda as well. They're coming tomorrow for cards."

That night, I witnessed what was to be the last stage of Edna's transformation—Edna, who'd insulated herself in our cottage, began dusting the living room and wiping down the windows, readying our place for guests. I ran the vacuum over the carpet and did a few other things, all the while wondering at how her mood had lifted itself into an airy satisfaction. She'd had a good day, she said, had written four pages, remembered almost every strategy in her card book. It was only when I was straightening the mail table that I found her articles hidden beneath old magazines. She had maybe twenty or so, Xeroxed, with notes in the margins. I saw them only briefly, but long enough to realize many explained experimental stem cell procedures that might help elderly patients who experienced difficulties of the mind.

We went to bed rather late, after a glass of wine apiece, and lay there for a while, the moonlight slanting in through our window, the extra comforter on our bed against the cold. She did something she hadn't done in weeks; she curled next to me in our nest of blankets. I can think of few things as sweet as that, Edna's body pushed against mine, her head on my chest. Before we surrendered to sleep, she told me how surprised she was to learn that her friends had missed her. They'd talked for hours, the four of them. Just before nodding off, she told me something Linda had said: "She thought she saw Mr. Reeve move his right arm." But I didn't say anything, scared of ruining this moment. I simply folded her in my arms and closed my eyes.

That night I was lowered into sleep gradually, passing through a spacious darkness, until I recognized that I was in a dream. I stood in a dim replica of my own cottage, the walls slightly darker, the windows filled with the gray sunlight of winter. Edna was with me, writing at our table, but she wasn't writing in her journal. She was writing a letter to her mother who had died over twenty years ago. The dream was fluid, like water flowing into me, and through this I understood Edna could remember every detail of her life, the first dress she wore at junior high, the names she'd once picked for our hypothetical children. As I walked out the front door, I moved like a young man, a mercurial smoothness oiled into my knees and arms. Before me were lovely plants in bloom, icicle succulents with flowers the colors of which I have never seen. I turned to regard the Reeves' estate. Horses were once again in his yard, along with the long, steel trailer Mr. Reeve had used to transport them, and then I found Mr. Reeve himself, standing on his front lawn, playing soccer with his son.

I felt such a deep peace in my dream I was unwilling to leave it. When the sun woke me, I closed my eyes hoping to sample the dream's emotions again. Gradually I became aware of coffee, the day's warmth on my face, soft music coming from our kitchen.

That morning I had my usual breakfast of toast and coffee, but for some reason Edna had decided to eat inside, abandoning our practice of watching the Reeves' estate. Instead she read up on card games. I returned to my habit of reading the newspaper, but it didn't capture my interest. I had only a minor curiosity about problems in the Middle East and even less in the financial markets that day. I left Edna as she dressed for town—she wanted refreshments to serve—and wandered out into the Collinses' yard only to find the ground had frozen over.

The air was much colder than it had been all month, but I liked the effect it had on me, its briskness. Clouds stretched across the horizon. The mountains were capped with snow. I performed the first of my winter duties—salting the long drive leading to the garage. I also switched on an outdoor heater designed to keep the fish pond from freezing. I spent a good deal of the morning blowing leaves from the lawn. Still I had time to check on the Reeves' estate.

Around ten I found Mr. Reeve on his porch, his wife working his arms, stretching one then the other. How I wanted him to move his arms, to lift his elbow just a quarter inch. But even I could see how useless his body was to him, his limbs that of a marionette. I watched as she finished the exercises. Eventually she wheeled her husband into their house, but I could not see inside that day as their windows were thick with fog.

I worked for a while in the side yard, blowing leaves, then returned to the cottage. I expected Edna would say something about my early arrival, but she was caught up in her own activities. She'd covered the kitchen table with a red cloth and set about making finger sandwiches. I helped for a while, setting out the odd candle and uncapping a bottle of cinnamon oil she liked to burn when we had company. I tried to be my best self—she appeared so pleased to have friends over—so after kissing her cheek, I returned to the yard, rake in hand, and began to straighten up the front as well.

I considered the nature of hope—what harm could it do anyone? After a while I felt a little better, believing Edna was happier now than she'd been last month or the month before. But still my attention kept drifting to the Reeves' estate. Once I saw William walk across the front, a garden hose coiled around his shoulder. Another time I saw a flock of birds settle in an elm before continuing south. Just after one o'clock I saw two men with medical satchels enter the Reeves' property, but I couldn't see inside. Shortly thereafter I made my way back to the cottage.

After lunch, Edna swept off our porch. In truth, I believe this was more out of nervousness than any desire to clean. As she stood there, the broom in her hands, I saw her glance at the Reeves' house, only to find Mr. and Mrs. Reeve on their porch accompanied by the two doctors. These doctors talked to the Reeves, their faces serious, their leather cases resting by their feet. Even from this distance, I could tell that Mrs. Reeve was upset, her lips thin, her hand set on her husband's shoulder. They had obviously captured Edna's attention; she set the broom against our cottage and moved into the yard so she might better see our neighbors.

I joined her there, beside a sugar pine that Mr. Collins used to decorate with lights. I sensed the sorrow of this moment, an odd weight I remembered feeling moments before Edna had told me about the ovarian cysts. Even though I couldn't hear a single word that passed between the Reeves and their doctors, I knew what was happening. I would have given anything to shield Edna, to prevent her from seeing this with me. We watched as one doctor—the taller one—lifted Mr. Reeve's arm, much as we'd seen his wife do, and then used his other hand to probe the muscles. The doctor held the arm for a long time—minutes, it seemed—moving it this way and that, before finally returning it to Mr. Reeve's lap, a gesture undeniably final. The doctors talked for a minute more before retrieving their satchels. Neither shook Mrs. Reeve's hand good-bye.

Edna went back inside, leaving the broom on the porch, while I remained in the yard. I felt the good mood of the last two weeks slip from us. How much time did she have before the effects were noticeable? Five years? Seven? We would be in our seventies then. I regretted all the time I'd lose with her and I didn't want to lose these last good years as well. I wanted someone to take this sadness from us, the knowledge that Edna would never be her old self again, not fully, that she'd lose a little bit more each year, even if that loss could be slowed by pills.

When I returned to the cottage, I expected to find her in the dark of our bedroom, writing in her journal or obsessively sorting old photographs. Instead I found her at the kitchen table, a glass of punch by her hand. She was wearing the dress she'd bought earlier that week, olive with brown stitchwork, and her hair was pulled back with a wooden clip. She was considering the rest of her life—or so I believed. If a man as rich as Mr. Reeve couldn't get these cells to work for him, how would they ever work for her? After her initial diagnosis, she'd spent a good deal of time alone, either in the kitchen or the bedroom, but now I saw something else in her. I thought she was sensing the life that was still inside her, the turn of good hope we'd experienced this week.

For these reasons—or for others I might never know—she did something I didn't expect. She lifted the cards from their plastic case and began to shuffle them. I sat beside her, my knee touching hers, our bodies perched on two wooden chairs, side by side. Dim light slanted in through our windows. Our house was filled with the vague fragrance of cinnamon oil. She dealt us each seven cards, but I left mine on the table. She turned, such a depth in her eyes I wondered at it—I believed she was deciding right then who she'd be for the rest of her life—and I understood the next moment to be crucial in a way few moments ever are. Slowly her features began to soften, first her eyes, then her mouth, then she looked at her cards, noticing the hand she'd dealt herself. "I thought we could play a couple hands," she said. "I'd like to practice before the ladies get here at three."

Newsworld

Every time I saw Thom Jenks, fellow employee at Newsworld, my heart flapped around in my chest like a fish. I forgot to breathe he looked so good—tall and casual, hair so thick women would come up to him and say, "I'd kill to have hair like that." I was twenty-one that year, and Thom was twenty-one as well, a college kid on break. We worked the afternoon shift at a ride called Watergate Hotel: The Break-In. He'd stand in the hot Georgia sun, dressed like a White House intern, starched shirt and thin maroon tie. "How many in your party?" he'd ask. Then I'd seat the guests in a reportermobile, two in front, three in back, check their lap bars before sending them swerving into a one-fifth scale replica of the Watergate Hotel circa 1970.

Needless to say, my family had always been interested in the news. After my father lost his job as a security officer in the aerospace industry, he'd spent his afternoons at home watching the cable news channel, sometimes with other men laid off from his company. Even after he took a job at the mall, he still watched both the national and the local broadcast each night while my mother fixed dinner in the kitchen. My own connection to the news is not as easy to define: when I was a freshman in high school I attempted to write for the school paper but discovered I wasn't good at reporting events with words. Instead I produced detailed line drawings of varsity athletes in action and of guest speakers who visited our school. By the end of my freshman year I'd produced two full pads. Seeing my work in print, I felt a sense of usefulness I hadn't known before.

I was sixteen when my parents started fighting. Most nights I stayed in my room, reworking my drawings while they bickered in the kitchen. But one night after my father retreated to our screened-in porch, I sat with him. Gesturing toward the edge of our weedy lawn, he told me that he felt a larger life somewhere out there, a life he wanted me to find. He tapped cigar ash into a saucer he balanced on his knee, then turned to me, his eyes soft and steady in the glow of our porch light. "When I was young I liked to think about the space industry," he said, "but space is no longer important. The public has become disenchanted with the future. It no longer matters to them." He put his hand on my shoulder, a rare gesture. "Find something meaningful to do, but something useful as well. It'll help you in the long run, a job like that." He smiled thoughtfully then blew smoke out the corner of his mouth before his eyes again settled on me. "Tell me you understand what I'm saying."

"Yes," I said, "I do."

The following year he died in a car accident, and the year after that I entered art school, my admissions portfolio consisting of line drawings I'd completed for my school paper as well as a few color sketches of houses damaged by a local hurricane. Without exception, my professors preferred my work with the hurricane. When asked their reasons, they pointed to the perspective and the use of color. Then one lowered his gaze to meet mine. "We all remember that storm," he said. "It had quite an impact on us."

For a while, as a student, I wanted to teach studio art in high school, but then I realized I would not make a good teacher. Some months later I considered a career as a courtroom sketch artist. But while enrolled in a course called Social Vision and the Artist, my father's advice returned to me. Almost overnight I saw a larger life out there, something beyond simple courtroom artistry. The following summer I began my career at Newsworld.

For weeks I tried not to look at Thom. I was still telling myself I wasn't full-time gay, only kind-of gay, like James Dean or Mick Jagger. But I was aware of him—at times intensely so. I knew the rhythm of his feet as he shuffled across the salmon-colored cement outside the entrance to our ride. When I worked the line, I found myself imitating the precise, almost military manner with which he held the counter, clicking off each guest who entered. One evening at the local mall, I spent twenty minutes spraying cologne on sample cards, hoping to find his exact scent, until the sales clerk suggested I leave. The next day I gave myself permission to look at him from time to time, to stare at him really, as he greeted guests and sent them down the velvet ropes toward me.

He was in town for the summer, I soon learned, a prelaw student studying in Boston, but a local at heart, an Atlanta boy. I could stand in the employee parking lot for hours with him, drinking sodas we'd purchased from the vending machine, talking about nothing other than Newsworld gossip and movies we wanted to see. We spent three nights in a row like that, leaning against his VW Rabbit as the moon lifted off the horizon and buttered us with its golden light.

We kissed for the first time the following week, a Wednesday. We were supposed to leave the park immediately after our shift, but he talked me into staying. We took off our ties, ran our cards through the time clock. We reentered at 1950s Square, just as blue-and-white lights flickered on in park trees like thousands of staticky pixels and the Newsworld Players began their reenactment of the McCarthy trials on a raised wooden stage. We walked through World War II Land and past a life-sized reconstruction of the Berlin Wall, which for a dollar a slug guests could chip away at with a sledgehammer. Eventually we ended up in the park's newest attraction, Tiananmen Square: The Revolt. We sat in stadium-style theater seats, our shoulders touching, while stage actors dressed as Beijing students reenacted their famous rebellion. Toward the show's climax, as one lone student faced off against a tank, I saw something in Thom I'd never seen before, an intensity in his expression. Eyes hazy, he turned to me. I believe he'd intended to reveal some insight about the way this show was orchestrated, but stopped, his lips slightly parted, holding back words. He looked at me for a long time, then kissed me—a soft, tentative kiss—before turning back to the stage, where the actor-students threw rocks at the Chinese troops advancing on them.

We fell in love slowly, stealing kisses inside the Watergate Hotel, letting our hands touch as we ate lunch in the employee break area. Thom had had three boyfriends before me—serious college boyfriends. I'd never had someone who bought me gifts or slipped notes into my employee locker. I'd never held hands in public—not with a boy, anyway—and was nervous as we walked around the park, not wanting to create a scene. Only once were we caught, the two of us hidden inside a Cold War silo, my hand folded over his. Our boss, Mandy Swanson, smiled then walked away.

The previous summer Thom had worked for Bill Clinton's reelection campaign. After graduation he wanted to settle down, have a life partner, and maybe adopt a kid. "All those normal things," he told me. When I told him I wanted to stay at Newsworld and work in development, he looked at me as though I didn't understand something essential about my own aspirations.

"This is just a summer job," he explained.

"I want to work here full time. You know, in Planning."

He remained beside me, seated on my secondhand sofa, trying to hide his confusion.

There was only one thing I could do. I retrieved my sketch pad from under the coffee table so he could see what I'd been working on for the past two years: concept drawings for new attractions I planned to someday show park executives. I showed him stage panels for an attraction I called Gulf War: The Attack and another for LA Riots: Flashpoint of Violence. For LA Riots I envisioned guests seated in the open bay of a fire truck as it raced through riot-torn Los Angeles en route to a warehouse fire. My panels showed the truck sprinting past a strip mall surrounded by mechanized looters, past gang members overturning cars in a parking lot, past an apartment building where elderly people trembled behind windows. After the truck arrived at the fire, guests were offloaded into a postshow area where an animated mannequin dressed to resemble Rodney King repeated segments of his "Can We All Get Along" speech every ninety seconds.

Thom studied my drawings for a long time, occasionally glancing at me, a half-empty wine glass poised in his hand. "This is a thrill ride," he said.

"It incorporates elements of a thrill ride," I corrected, "into a news-oriented attraction." I closed my sketchpad and tucked it under my arm. "I always thought my father would've been interested in it."

He turned to me, confusion evident in his expression.

"It's a larger life," I explained, "presenting the news in a way that makes people feel more involved with it."

We sat there for a moment, neither of us talking. "Your father," he finally said, "did he understand about you?"

"In some ways."

He looked to the window briefly, then turned back to me. "My father didn't really understand me either," he said.

That night Thom stayed at my apartment. We finished the wine and started kissing, little pecks on the cheek then neck, before we lay side by side on the couch. Eventually we went to my bedroom, but even there I wasn't confident enough to undress him without relying on some nonsexual pretext. I rolled him on to my mattress, mock-wrestling until he buckled me into an embrace, his arms pinning me with a delicate half nelson, then kissed me softly on the lips. I answered him by untucking his shirt and placing my hands on his bare back. I was amazed at the softness, the outline of his spine like tiny stones covered with silk.

Hours later I lay beside him, the sheets damp with exhaustion, enjoying a breeze from my ceiling fan. We were quiet for a long time, looking at the city lights through my window. Finally he asked to see my sketchpad again. I explained each panel, narrating the story I hoped to tell through this ride. Afterward he looked at me, his eyes deep and curious, his expression so thoughtful I knew he understood something important about me, about the feelings of sadness I carried inside. He put his hand on my shoulder so gently I didn't feel his touch at first. Though he didn't much like Newsworld, his voice was sympathetic when he said, "You really believe in this?"

"Most everyone watches the news. It's one of the few things that connect us." He was so beautiful, his dark eyes, the stubble peppered on his chin, his cheeks tan like the color of toast. "One of the few things that connects us *as a nation,*" I added.

In the days that followed, I caught him looking at attractions such as The Vietnam Experience and Hostages in Iran in such a quiet, contemplative manner I believed he was reconsidering their cultural importance. Likewise, when we were alone, I noticed a new sadness in him, a sadness I liked to believe came from the knowledge that our love wouldn't extend beyond the summer. He became gentle with me, placing his hand on my shoulder as we walked to break, occasionally bringing a six-pack of sodas, which we hid just inside the Watergate Hotel.

I told myself I didn't care that he was leaving. That was how the adult world worked: people came together then moved apart. Only at night did I feel the impending loss, when he was at my apartment watching cable and drinking merlot. I enjoyed his company, the smart things he said about people at work, the way he looked at me from across the room. Two or three times a week he spent the night, bundled onto the small raft of my bed, our bodies covered by a single cotton sheet. I hooked my arm around his middle as his breathing became slow and night tremors rippled through the thin frame of his chest.

On the day he left, I said goodbye to him at his mother's apartment, then watched his car, loaded with clothes and books, move slowly beneath the parkway trees and toward the freeway. Only when I was by myself, driving home, did I finally feel the emptiness. I spent the night watching Wolf Blitzer on CNN, though in truth I was thinking of Thom, his arrival in Boston, his old friends, the two-bedroom apartment he rented near campus.

At first I wrote every day, mostly to update him on park gossip—for example, our boss was now dating the manager of Siege at Waco—but by the end of the second week, I'd received only three letters from him, short greetings that detailed his life at school. On the phone I sensed his excitement as he talked about social activities he attended with his friends. Even though he suggested I visit, his voice didn't sound as sincere as it had over the summer. When I said I was too busy to go to Boston, he did not argue as I'd hoped. Instead he said, "Maybe we can meet up next semester." Following that, I talked to him only twice, short calls punctuated with silence, until I understood he wished to move beyond our summer relationship and fall more completely into his life at school. After I hung up, I stood at my window, hands locked behind my back, and wondered if I'd missed some clue that would've told me how this would end.

¤

I devoted the better part of that year to my studies. I took my final courses in drawing and mixed media but spent most of my time finishing my senior portfolio, detailed renderings of the show buildings I planned for Newsworld. Each time my major professor looked at my work, his eyes glazed over, perhaps remembering other nontraditional students who'd come before me. More than once he advised against the entertainment industry. "I know some people who work in the courtroom," he told me. "I could arrange something for you."

At Newsworld I was doing my best to be a model part-time employee, arriving early and staying late. I regularly filled out employee suggestion forms, noting small ways the park might improve, such as better color design for its rides and signposts directing guests to out-of-the-way attractions. Every other Friday I took on the role of mentor, helping to train new employees. I took these recruits from Personnel over to the uniform office, then to 1950s Square, where I explained the basic layout of the park: guests entered through The Gates of the Twentieth Century and worked their way through chronologically placed attractions until they reached the final shop called Gifts for the Coming Millennium.

At the end of orientation, new employees inevitably asked about my own role at Newsworld. At first I told them I was a part-time ride operator, but as I grew more comfortable I confided my dream of designing attractions. A few times, I opened a plastic portfolio to show them storyboards for my proposed LA Riots ride.

After I returned to Personnel one afternoon, I met Daniel Yardley, a tall, thin man with wavy hair. Officially Daniel was supposed to check in my mentor materials as well as file the employee uniform requests

I'd asked each new recruit to complete, but on that day he was somewhat chatty. He was telling me about a new bar down in the Buckhead district when he noticed the plastic portfolio wedged under my arm. "You're the one in art school, aren't you?"

I was, I told him.

"And you want to design rides?"

"Concept art," I explained, "and things like that. Maybe some model work. I'm not trained as an engineer."

"Yes, yes," he said, as though he understood the difference. With two fingers he tugged at my portfolio. "Are these your drawings?" His eyes lanced toward mine, and he must have noticed something about me, my reluctance perhaps.

Somewhat embarrassed, I removed my boards from their sheath and placed them on the counter in proper order. I had only five panels with me, one for each of the five stages in my LA Riots ride. Daniel examined each, noting little details, such as a television news van parked in the distance and a street vendor's cart turned on its side. From the way he held them, the boards pinched between his fingers, I believed he liked my work a great deal. "These are better than I thought they'd be," he said. "Not that I didn't think they'd be good. You know what makes these so good?"

"No."

"Realism," he continued. "These drawings look realistic. That's what's missing from the park, a sense of realism." He placed his hand on my arm. "I mean, I can see this ride as a real event, something that actually happened at some point in history. I never get this feeling from the rides we have now."

"I kind of like the rides now."

"They're interesting in their own way, like a child's introduction to the twentieth century, but they don't have the sense of realism I get from your drawings." Only then did I notice his hand was still on my arm. "Say, I'm meeting some people down in Buckhead tonight. You have plans?"

Out of habit, I replied, "I'm busy," but immediately regretted it. I left quietly, looking back only once to see him seated at his desk, dressed in a striped button-down, the sleeves rolled neatly to his elbows.

¤

Over the week that followed, I used my employee pass privileges to attend the park on the nights I was not scheduled to work. I reviewed each ride in a systematic manner, noting that what Daniel had said was true: almost every ride was designed to provide a young adult's introduction to a major news story. How could I have not seen this before? The Vietnam Experience did little more than recreate the cartoonish landscape of war in an outdoor show area, presenting two companies of American soldiers and a few Vietcong camouflaged with leaves and mud. Great Moments with Martin Luther King offered a three-minute abridgment of his famous "I Have a Dream" speech. Even the attraction where I worked, Watergate Hotel: The Break-In, was riddled with oversimplification: Woodward and Bernstein moved clumsily through a hallway, Nixon sat behind his presidential desk shaking his head in disgust. None of these attractions even sought to explore the complexities of the original story as it had been presented on TV.

Slowly I began to rework all of the drawings for my LA Riots ride, noting ways I might heighten the realism of each stage and at the same time present a complex rendition of the actual news story. True, I was limited by the traditional boundaries of a dark ride—I only had a few minutes, at most a half mile of track—but still I believed I could do a better job than those designers who had come before me. I wanted to create a ride that would appeal to the adults who had lived through the event, as well as younger guests who had not seen the coverage on TV.

In my original version, each stage for LA Riots had illustrated a separate aspect of the event. For example, on one stage I'd constructed a scene depicting group lootings. On another, two individuals set fire to a TV repair shop. Artificial, I now saw. Totally artificial. Instead I decided to merge these stages together into one continuous scene, the events happening simultaneously, much as they would've during the actual riots.

At work I began to leave critical comments in the employee suggestion box, some of which asked park managers to revamp the Watergate Hotel. I wanted the Republican office to be larger, more completely furnished. I wanted the models of Woodward and Bernstein, created with the mechanics available in the early 1980s, to be replaced with state-of-the-art models, ones that had a greater range of facial expression and individual finger movement. Most of all I wanted the ride transformed into a walk-through attraction much like The Vietnam Experience. Reportermobiles, what were those? In my own design for the LA Riots ride, I used hollowed-out fire engines as the means of guest transport. Yes, hollowed-out fire engines weren't entirely true-to-life, but at least fire engines had been present during the actual riots.

Not surprisingly, Daniel became my biggest supporter, since all comments dropped into the employee suggestion box were routed through Personnel. Occasionally we would meet for lunch in the employees' break area, where I showed him revisions for my LA Riots ride. He seemed impressed, even though these drawings were simply rendered in pencil. Often he asked to show them to other people he knew in Personnel. At the end of June, a VP named Edie Jones bumped into me outside the employee lockers. "You're the one interested in ride development," she said.

"Art direction and design," I said. "Yes."

"I've read your comments about the park. Very critical."

"I don't mean to be. I just think certain attractions could be more realistic and make better use of the dimensional space. With a bit of tinkering, new attractions could attract more adult guests."

"More adult guests?" she repeated. She reached into her pocket and removed a business card. Like all Newsworld cards, it included an ink drawing of the park mascot, a squirrel holding a magnifying glass up to its right eye. "Look" she said, "I'm very busy this week, but I'd like you to call me at my office. People have told me about your drawings."

Later that month I graduated from art school, fifth in my class. During the ceremony I sat next to a man who'd animated a short S&M version of Pinocchio as his senior project, called *Pinocchio, the Big Fag*. Dressed in my cap and gown, I waited patiently for my name to be called, all the while looking out into the dim pit of the audience, where my mother sat with her new boyfriend. She lived in Charlotte now. When my name was called, I walked to center stage and received my degree bound by a loop of red ribbon. I shook the hand of my advisor, who greeted me with the same glassy expression he used on all new graduates, as though dismissing each to certain failure.

Afterward my mother and her boyfriend took me out for an early dinner. Repeatedly she told me how proud she was of my accomplishments, how much my father would have wanted to see me on this very special day. More than once I tried to explain my senior project to her, my concept drawings for rides at Newsworld, but she never seemed to understand their importance, how design elements in my work challenged the existing approach to virtually every ride at the park. When I told her about my possible promotion, she placed her hand on my back and said, "I'm glad you found a job you like."

The following day, while my mother and her boyfriend brunched at their hotel, I drove aimlessly around Atlanta, down freeways and busy streets, until I arrived at Newsworld. I sat in my car for at least ten minutes before I began to walk around the employees' break area. From where I stood, I could make out the park's skyline: tall attractions, such as Voyage of the Titanic, rising above boundary trees. I drank two diet sodas from a vending machine, then sat at a bus stop with other employees. Eventually I walked to the back lot—past Costuming and Landscaping, until I happened upon Personnel. Even though it was Sunday I saw a light on, a dim glow behind tinted windows. I cupped my hands so I could better see inside. There at his desk, Daniel was processing a stack of employee uniform requests. He looked so official, his hair combed back, his shirt buttoned to his collar. Eventually he saw me, with my hands like small wings attached to the sides of my face.

"Is there something wrong?" he asked.

"I'm just having a bad day," I said. "I thought I might see you."

He stood in the doorway, momentarily confused, then stepped aside. "Why don't you come in," he said.

¤

I suppose I'd been falling in love with Daniel for months, only I'd been too involved with my own senior project to notice. After I began my new job as an assistant in Park Planning, I found myself hand-delivering forms to Personnel that I could have easily sent through inside mail. I parked in the lot nearest his building instead of using the lot reserved for Planning. During my lunch break I took to wandering the park under the guise of surveying rides, but usually I ended up near Personnel, where I saw him talking to other men. Mostly these men were ride operators, just as I'd been, neatly dressed in their uniforms. Each time I saw him he said hello, but his tone had changed, no longer holding his earlier ease and warmth.

In Park Planning I worked with Jack Spears, a senior designer. I was not yet allowed to contribute directly; my duties included checking other artists' work for both color accuracy and scale. Ideally, art from the Planning Department gave engineers a good idea of a ride's design and overall appearance, while at the same time generating public interest in a new attraction. Concept drawings and architectural renderings regularly appeared in stockholders' reports and the local paper, often alongside three-dimensional work from our model shop.

At the time I was hired, Planning was assembling the storyboards for an OJ Simpson ride called OJ's Bronco: Final Pursuit. Guests rode along in a Ford Bronco past a replica of Nicole Brown Simpson's condominium, then OJ's Rockingham estate, before finally joining a freeway pursuit that concluded with OJ surrendering to police custody. At the bottom of each drawing, in a decorative tea-script, was the updated Newsworld slogan: "Commemorating the News Moments of our Lives."

I saw my job in a simple light. I wanted to increase the realism of each drawing. I spent hours reviewing news footage and scouring articles stored on microfilm. I noted small details, such as the type of flowers stacked at Nicole Brown Simpson's condo and the missing sections of her white picket fence that some onlooker had stolen as a souvenir. Occasionally I redid a senior artist's sketch, adding my own details, such as autograph hounds outside OJ's estate and homeless men camped beside the freeway. Just as often, I sent a color Xerox to Daniel, but rarely did I hear back, except for little notes that said "Thanks" or "Looks interesting." No longer did he analyze my work or offer suggestions, not even when I told him his opinion really mattered to me.

As it turned out, Jack liked my work, especially my attention to historic detail, but often felt my stage arrangement was overpowering. "You need to remember a ride is a lot like a movie. You need to frame the experience scene by scene, building the story."

"But that's just it," I said. "I want the ride to convey the chaos of reality. I'm striving for multiple points of focus."

Jack considered this, folding his big, baggy hands into his lap and bending over my sketches one more time. He was a cautious, exacting man, often enthusiastic about young artists' work. He'd trained other well-known ride design artists, such as Tad Herman and Rhonda Collins, both of whom had already left Newsworld for jobs in central Florida. From his expression, I understood he did not yet understand my vision, that full-fare adult guests were ready for a more complex presentation of important news stories like that of OJ Simpson. "Why don't you redo your stages so they hold two or three points of focus? I think you might get somewhere with that."

Though I believed this was only an academic exercise, I went back to my cubicle and removed a fresh sheet of vellum. Using a light box, I traced my presentation of Nicole Brown Simpson's condominium, limiting the points of focus to just three: a crowd of onlookers/grievers, two vandals slyly removing the numbers from her mailbox and three officers remarking the barrier with yellow police tape. Gradually I saw how this was a compromise between the old Newsworld style and a more conscious approach to realism. Also, I saw how creating the illusion of chaos—while in fact manipulating guests' attention—might better control the elements of storytelling implicit in such a ride.

That afternoon I redid my stage of the Rockingham estate using a similar approach, then tinkered with the highway pursuit—a fairly standard set piece that was easy to break into dramatic vignettes. But even here, I was able to promote a historicity absent from so many Newsworld attractions. I included actual handwritten banners onlookers had hung from overpasses. I added one-third-scale models of TV news helicopters heading with the police caravan toward the gray mass of the LA foothills. The ride eventually let out in a walk-through exhibition hall where the mechanical figure of DA Gil Garcetti asked guests to review the evidence, both for and against OJ, and come to their own verdict.

I was well into my seventh sketch when I noticed that the entire office had gone dark except for my cubicle. Through my second-story window, I could see into 1950s Square, where the nightly parade was turning onto Eisenhower Lane, led as always by an actor who resembled JFK, seated in the backseat of a black convertible. Only then, as I rose from my desk, did I hear the soft sound of a man breathing. I turned to find Daniel, dressed in his striped button-down and khakis, sleeves rolled to his elbows. He appeared tired, one arm hooked casually over my cubicle wall.

"Your work's still very good," he said.

His sandy hair, usually perfectly combed, was falling into his face.

"Don't worry," he said. "I've only been here a minute. But I like watching you. You look transported when you draw." From his breast pocket he unfolded a note I'd written to him some two or three weeks ago. "Is this what you meant," he asked, "that my opinion matters to you?"

"Of course your opinion matters."

"No," he corrected. "Did you intend to say something more?"

I noticed now that his eyes were veined with tiny red lines and his face was dotted with perspiration. "I thought you were seeing other men," I said. He stood stiffly, thumbs tucked into his belt. He smelled of mixed drinks. I took his hand in my own. Though I expected a certain electricity, instead I felt a warm, calming sensation. "I meant to say a lot more," I said. We stood there, doing nothing other than holding hands, his body a good distance from mine.

¤

Daniel was shy. Despite his experience in bars, he was somewhat awkward when we were alone. We talked quietly in restaurants and coffee shops, our fingers touching under the table. He'd worked in Personnel for three years, I found out, and hoped to become a personnel officer. "Either at Newsworld," he said, "or a large hotel." He liked clubs but not dancing. He liked foreign movies but not if they were dubbed. He liked his hometown, but liked Atlanta as well.

Each time we were alone, he expected me to make the first move. Often while we watched cable, I'd put my arm around his shoulders. In ways I was perfectly content sitting beside him, *The Late Show* or *Headline News* flickering on TV, but I understood what he desired. Occasionally he'd wrestle me, much in the manner I'd wrestled Thom, our own mock struggle, but he wanted me to embrace him, to bring him close in such a way as to make our mood turn serious. Slowly I learned how to give these things to him, by unbuttoning his shirt in a gradual, teasing way, running my hand across the smooth plane of his chest. Each time I offered these gestures, I felt some spirit inside me expand, some warmth that told me I was falling more deeply in love.

On those nights when he slept over, I woke early, often before 5:00 a.m., to sit in my breakfast nook reworking individual character details for the OJ ride. I drew panel after panel of onlookers/grievers arranged outside of Nicole Brown Simpson's condo, giving them expressions of emotional depth absent from most every figure in a Newsworld attraction. I worked with light and shadow. I tried to color up each scene so that it held the muted tones of video footage presented on a standard TV.

One morning, a month or so into our relationship, Daniel sat beside me, his hand curved around a coffee mug, as I roughed out the frustrated expression of one police detective. We were dressed in pajama boxers and T-shirts, both of us a little groggy as the morning sun slanted through my kitchen window. He stayed with me a long time, maybe half an hour, not saying anything, not even when he refilled our cups. After a time, I stopped thinking of my work and began to consider our relationship. I asked myself how many people would I let sit beside me while I drew? The answer was easy. I'd let no one else sit there—only Daniel.

I kissed him on the cheek.

"What's that for?" he asked.

"Just because."

"Just because *what?*"

That day I brought butter toffee peanuts to him at Personnel, the kind they sold at vending carts inside the park. After work I met him in the parking lot, where my car was parked next to his. When I saw him around the break area checking on new employees, I noticed he no longer flirted with young men but instead kept a professional distance and often directed their attention to papers he'd brought with him. In short, he'd settled into a more mature, career-minded version of himself. He began to wear gray sport jackets over his striped shirts. He kept business cards in his wallet. Twice a week he called the personnel director to check on projects he might do in his spare time. He attended conferences on regional tourism. He followed the quarterly report and inspected press packets. Because of this, Daniel was the first person I knew to see my work in print.

Unknown to me, the second-quarter report featured one of my drawings, a cutaway done with colored pencil I'd given Jack two months earlier. In it, I'd presented a Ford Bronco loaded with six park guests as it passed Nicole Brown Simpson's condo. Surprisingly, it included my tri-focus presentation: the officers, the onlookers, the vandals. When I asked Jack about its publication he closed his office door. "Yes, that panel," he said. "It's good."

"It's in the quarterly report."

"I didn't know about the report until today. That's a surprise for me as well. The truth is, I've been talking to some people on the Oversight Committee. It seems they agree with you, the OJ attraction could expand toward adult realism. They like some of your ideas about multiple-focus stages as well."

"They do?"

"They do," he confirmed. "But don't get too excited. The Oversight

Committee is very traditional. I don't think they're ready to completely overhaul standard ride design just yet." He put a congratulatory hand on my shoulder. "I think it's about time you started attending weekly meetings with the other park planners."

That night Daniel took me to a Mediterranean restaurant and ordered a bottle of French champagne. He was happy for me, but I could tell he was somewhat upset as well. We talked about my promotion, how I'd become the youngest artist to attend oversight meetings in over twenty years, yet when I asked about his successes in Personnel, he turned quiet. He told me everything in Personnel was fine, that his boss was supportive of his work. Shortly before our main course arrived, he said, "Let's just talk about you tonight. You've wanted this for years."

After dessert we walked along the busy city streets, listening to the music coming from dance clubs, but Daniel was not interested in visiting bars where he once drank with his friends. Instead he wanted me to take him home. We made love in my full-sized bed, wisps of moonlight stenciled around us. Afterward I lay beside him, my fingers curved over his hip, holding him to me. I looked at the ceiling for a long time, noticing phosphorescent specks embedded into the paint, before I finally fell asleep, our bodies twinned under the sheet.

I woke early, perhaps 4:00 a.m., but instead of following my usual routine, I emptied half of the medicine cabinet, quietly removing old bottles of hair gel and cologne. I attached a handwritten note to the empty shelves: "Your things can go here." I looked at him lying in my bed, his arm hooked over a pillow, and I wondered what it would feel like to have him around me always. I liked the emotion in that fantasy but was scared by it as well. I touched his shoulder softly then left the room for the office, so he could consider my offer in private.

He found me before the work day actually began while I was standing outside my cubicle. He approached slowly, dressed in a striped shirt and jacket. I could not read his expression. His face was pensive, as it often was at work, but when he was close, his lips widened into a cautious smile. "Are you sure this is what you want?" he asked.

"It is," I said.

He took my hand, a gesture I understood to be a question. I answered by reaching for his other hand. We stood there for at least a minute until Jack Spears and two other managers entered through the main office doors, causing us to separate out of habit.

¤

Daniel moved in slowly, transferring his clothes one suitcase at a time: work clothes first, then casual shirts and shorts. He sold a few of his household possessions, such as his microwave and refrigerator, as well as the golf clubs he'd bought five years ago. I removed a number of framed photos from the living room so he'd feel the apartment was as much his as it was mine. I left only a single portrait of my parents and my art school diploma on the wall above the couch.

It took a week for him to settle in and another before he felt comfortable enough to leave his shoes by the front door. More than once, as we watched late-night talk shows, I caught him staring at me when he thought I wouldn't notice. Gradually I came to understand that there was something about me that perplexed him. "You could spend your whole life working for the park, couldn't you? Designing new rides?"

He was bathed in the iridescent glow of the TV. "It's not a bad job," I told him.

"But you love your work?"

"Yeah," I said, "I do."

He laid his hand on my back, one of the ways he initiated intimacy, so I kissed him softly on the lips. "If I had your single-mindedness, I'd be personnel director by now."

The following morning Daniel did something that surprised me:

while I worked on my drawings he began to rewrite sections of the employee handbook onto a legal pad. He worked slowly, crossing out words, reworking sentences until each paragraph had a clean, direct voice. By the time we took our showers, he'd finished two pages. The next day, he finished two more. Over the week that followed, I noticed small changes in the way he presented himself: he wore red silk ties; he buffed his shoes each night before bed; he carried a leather organizer tucked under the crook of his arm. In short, Daniel was modeling his professional appearance after my own.

At work I was given a new title, associate planner, and an office with a window overlooking the park. With the extra salary I bought new tweed blazers like those senior planners wore. I grew accustomed to having a shared secretary who kept track of my meetings and a clerk who handled my copying and office-supply needs.

Those months, I suppose, were the most satisfying of my life. I thought of Daniel in a new way, not simply as my companion but as a man I wanted to make happy. While driving to work I often imagined exactly what would give him that happiness. I bought him gifts— striped shirts and ties—but these seemed inadequate to express what I truly felt.

Sometimes as we sat together reading magazines or eating dinner, I felt an odd sorrow open inside of me, a sensation of such breadth I wondered why I'd never felt it before. When I told Daniel that these feelings were new to me, he simply laughed. "Only someone who went through art school would say that." So I began to see myself as entering regular adult life for the first time, shedding the last skin of my prolonged adolescence. Without realizing it, I memorized his habits and often imitated them: I squeezed toothpaste from the bottom of the tube, I turned on the dishwasher before going to bed, I used a small sponge to moisten the back of postage stamps. There were so many things I hadn't known about him, such as his secret love of classical music, his interest in TV shows about nature, and the way he hummed to himself while taking a shower.

Three times a week his mother called from Nebraska. She was a soft-spoken woman who'd once taught junior high. "So you're the man my son finally chose," she said.

"Yes, Mrs. Yardley, I'm the lucky man."

At work I noticed how other couples moved through this world of love, the little gestures they shared over coffee or lunch, and I began to suspect there was something about my own personality that had delayed this response until such a late age. Not surprisingly I felt a new confidence at work, a kinship with my fellow workers. With the exception of Terrance McNeal, the landscape architect, the other oversight members shared my enthusiasm to develop rides for an adult audience. Initially they were confused when I talked about the aesthetics of TV realism, but when I presented my drawings for the OJ ride, they uniformly agreed that this would be an interesting way to distinguish it from other Newsworld attractions.

Occasionally I had lunch with Beth Gundry from the Model Shop and Lance Peterson, a ride systems engineer. They were good people, I discovered, who felt the park was making a positive impact on local culture. Like me, they saw broadcast news as one of the dominant media forces in the coming millennium, and also like me, they wanted to be involved with it. We looked over each other's work: Lance had recently finished computer-generated wire models of the OJ Simpson ride vehicles, while Beth was finishing a clay model of Nicole Brown Simpson's condo.

Daniel, too, was finding success at work. Twice he was named Personnel Employee of the Month. He was given the responsibility of leading management orientations and promised a position as associate officer before the year's end. As we walked around the park, our shoulders almost touching, I felt a closeness to him that surprised me. I wanted him to do well in the world, to be happy, and though I had wanted other people to be happy, I'd never wanted it in exactly the same way I wanted it for him. Together we moved through the large show building where the construction team was beginning to lay down the first section of track for the OJ ride. We watched craftsmen create a replica of a Brentwood neighborhood using nothing more than cement, wood, fiberglass, and metal curved from a lathe, all of which would be painted according to the color-board specifications I'd completed the previous week. He looked at the stages as they were constructed, awed, as I was, that simple drawings could be transformed into something as tangible as these sets. We were in a world of our own design, Los Angeles circa 1994. As we stepped back into the harsh Georgia sun, we were both momentarily stunned to find ourselves inside a green construction fence, beside a cement truck and palettes of hay-colored bricks.

I expected the two of us to continue along this course, feathering our nest with small accomplishments, but soon after we celebrated Daniel's promotion he began to change, his earlier determination draining away. In the beginning these changes amounted to little: his decision not to wear a tie at work, his waning interest in corporate publications, the way he walked at work, a casual stride I remembered from our early months together. I saw him more regularly in the employee break area, talking to other young park officers, and twice I saw him in park gift shops, blankly staring at souvenir mugs and key chains engraved with the Newsworld logo.

By now I'd learned that not everyone loved their job as much as I did—or even could love it that way—and so I understood what was happening: he needed to distance himself from work. At home I was considerate. I watched the news only once, usually while he took a bath. After dinner I went to our bedroom while he flipped channels, looking for a show about nature or a courtroom drama.

After talking to Beth Gundry about my situation, I went out of my

way to set up special nights that had nothing to do with the park. I took
Daniel to movies at large cineplexes, noting his happiness as we sat in
the dark. I had a good time, too, eating popcorn, letting my body slant
against his. I hadn't seen a movie for months, in part because I believed
the art of Hollywood cinema had passed its peak. Entertainment in the
new millennium would be more closely derived from documentary: re-
ality-based TV shows, interactive museums and, of course, rides like
those we were building at the park. To finish our evenings out, we often
went to a bar, usually one Daniel had frequented during those weeks I
first knew him. As we entered he scanned the room for old friends, visibly disappointed to find no one he knew in attendance.

Despite my efforts, I could tell he was unhappy by the way he
looked at me across our kitchen table, confused and injured; by the way
he stared out our living room window watching cars pass on the street;
by the way he no longer sat beside me in the breakfast nook each morning. Still I felt that deep yearning to please him, that twisting inside my
chest. But now I noticed a new desire fused to it: I wanted him to ap-
preciate me, to acknowledge my efforts.

By the end of the summer we were bickering two or three nights a
week—about small matters mostly, such as what to watch on TV or the
way our toiletries were stored in the medicine cabinet. These arguments
made me think of those my parents had had when I was a teenager. I
began leaving the apartment at night to walk laps around our complex
or to sit by the pool. I'd never felt this alone, not even in high school
or after Thom had left. Why would I feel like this now? But then I remembered what my father had told me about the importance of having
a larger life.

I turned this idea over many times. All my life I'd believed my father had been offering general advice for a career, but now I wondered
if he'd sensed my coming failures at love. All those years ago, back on
our screened-in porch, had he known that men would leave me, that

I would need some special way to save myself from such loss? I didn't notice the air turn cold. I didn't notice the streetlights click off. I didn't even notice our security officer, Fred Bradley, enter the pool area. I was surprised when he tapped me on the shoulder. "You okay?"

I looked at him, confused, noticing the concern in his face.

"I think so," I said, "yeah."

I walked home slowly and got into bed beside Daniel, kissing him once on the cheek, but that kiss was different from all the kisses before it. I didn't need him to recognize me. I didn't need him to acknowledge the affection I was beginning to lose for him. In my dreams that night I was lowered by ropes to a platform far beneath my bed where, looking up, I could see myself lying beside Daniel, my body hunched toward his. And then, from deep within my dream consciousness, I willed myself to roll away and pull a pillow to my chest.

On the days that followed I went to work early, where I walked through the OJ ride, making notes on the relationship between my drawings and the sets as they now appeared. Certain expressions of emotion were absent in the figures outside Nicole Brown Simpson's condo. When the finishers from our Staging Department arrived, we discussed ways the figures could be more lifelike, their faces revealing the feelings I'd wanted them to have.

Daniel and I stopped fighting when I understood that we were not in love and perhaps hadn't been for some months. I believed he realized this, too—that we were merely companions. Though we spent a good deal of time apart, we ate dinner together two or three times a week, usually at a neighborhood restaurant. After some weeks had passed, he began talking to me in the slow, honest way I recalled from our earliest courtship. He told me he wasn't happy in Personnel, that he was tired of reviewing the same forms, having new employees ask the same questions. He'd stopped advancing because he no longer could see himself as the personnel director. "It's strange," he said. "When we first started going out, I thought I could be like you, that work could make me happy."

We looked at each other across a restaurant table, two plates of pasta between us.

"You're driven," he said. "That makes it hard to love you."

"I try not to be."

He let his gaze shift from me. "I know," he said.

¤

Even after we separated we talked often, usually in the employee break area, a place that would soon be bulldozed for a flight simulator attraction called Space Shuttle: The First Mission. We discussed bars and restaurants, how the park was attracting more adult guests. At times I felt the soft thrill of our old romance and remembered how much I'd enjoyed our early life together. More than once I thought of asking him on a date, hoping that we would fall in love again. But each time I lowered my voice into the register of intimate conversation, he looked away, as though the time for such a date had not yet arrived.

I continued to work in Park Planning, where managers were already suggesting I might have Jack Spears's office after he retired. With my close friends, such as Beth Gundry and Lance Peterson, I shared my sketches for a ride based on the LA Riots, though now I thought my original subtitle, Flashpoint of Violence, far too showy and artificial. Beth liked the idea of urban sets lit by fire and streetlights; Lance took to the challenge of ride vehicles using linear acceleration to provide an unexpected thrill. Gradually we talked to other members of the Oversight Committee so that when the ride concept was formally presented we'd have enough support to pass our proposal along for executive approval.

During those long summer nights, I walked through the Buckhead district, telling myself I was there to buy a book or perhaps foreign newspapers, but I always glanced in the bars Daniel had liked, ones with mahogany tables and dartboards on the wall. More than once I considered buying myself a drink, but I always went home, where I fell into the comfortable habit of drawing.

As the OJ ride neared completion, I took pleasure in taking members of the press behind the scenes to reveal the complex interworking of each stage. For the grand opening, I bought a new charcoal suit and new shoes. We had quite a turnout: *Good Morning America* and *The Today Show* arrived with video crews. I believed nothing could spoil my mood, but then, near the entrance to 1950s Square, I saw Daniel seated on a park bench beside a man with short blond hair. Their knees touched briefly then separated again. I looked at him for a long moment, wondering if I was reading the scene correctly. I turned away just in time to prepare myself for a cameraman and reporter approaching for another interview.

¤

That month I spent many evenings at the park, noting how guests responded to the OJ ride. I felt a certain satisfaction when adults rode it more than once, though afterward, at home, I experienced an emptiness inside my ribs, a sense of loneliness so strong I turned on the TV for company. I took to walking for exercise and even considered taking a design class at a local college. One night, I rehung all of my old photos, making the living room exactly as it had been before Daniel. I left them there for a week before I decided to take them down again.

On the day our LA Riots ride was given final approval, I went with Lance and Beth to the proposed site, a lot where parade floats were stored during the off-season. I felt much of my old excitement return, the sense of purpose I'd enjoyed when I'd first joined Planning. We paced off the perimeter of the proposed show building and discussed placement of the outdoor queue before taking our celebration to an Italian restaurant. After dinner, we sketched new show elements to be used in the ride: overturned cars, flames rising from apartment windows, water gushing from a hydrant at the end of a dark street.

It was after midnight when we noticed the restaurant empty, but I didn't want to go home just yet. Instead I walked by myself toward the pubs Daniel favored. I looked through the windows of the last establishment, but he wasn't there. Twenty or thirty people, most of them men, talked in small groups around the bar. I could go in, I understood, maybe talk with them. I was drawn to the excitement, but wary of it as well. I stood outside for a long time until I knew what I was supposed to do.

I walked home alone, keeping my hands in my pockets for warmth, but I felt different that night, as though I was finally moving beyond Daniel. A good feeling came down around me as I realized I'd be OK by myself. I was looking forward to designing this new ride—the drawings, the models, the way I'd work directly with the construction team. I could see the show stage so clearly now: the looters and police dressed in riot gear. In ways I fell into thoughts I'd first experienced back in art school, enjoying the comfort of them, believing that I was doing something important, creating rides that would be a testament to my own period of history and to the drama of human life we have all witnessed on TV.

Studio Sense

Early on I recognized my gift. In T-ball, the other children suggested I play shortstop, even though I had a slow arm and weak eyes. In both third and fourth grade, each candidate for class president asked me to be his running mate. For three consecutive years the drama teacher pushed lead roles my way. I refused them all. I wanted no part in such a life. I'd seen its effects all too clearly on my parents.

My father, a foreign investment banker, first met my mother while she was filming an episode of *Fantasy Island* that was financed in part by a bank in Grenada. They married quickly and just as quickly had me, their ornament, their child. In my early years, they often dressed me in suits and smoking jackets, scale replicas of my father's, then paraded me around parties for their guests to admire. In such moments my parents doted on me. I was their "Bukkums," their "Wonder Spud." But the following morning, while our maid cheerfully tipped ceramic ashtrays into the trash, I was returned to my role as the child who confused them, the unplanned child, the oft-mentioned apple of their eye, reminder that they were not above the world of regular people—the world of lawn care and carpools. Often my father would stand at the entrance to my play-room, a space that formerly had housed their extra clothes, and look at me with the fond, tired eyes of a man poorly prepared for fatherhood. "Wonder Spud," he might whisper, but without a toasty audience, his words lacked conviction. They were issued tentatively, a question.

In fairness, my parents were concerned with failure. My father had brokered many deals with South Pacific nationals that came to ruin. He had a hand in *Heaven's Gate, Airport '77,* and a short-lived spin-off of *Three's Company* called *The Ropers.* Despite my mother's lack of training, she'd managed to land parts on *The Love Boat, Hart to Hart,* and *Spenser: For Hire.* Her best known role was on *The Facts of Life,* where she played Mrs. Garrett's younger sister, Rhonda, for five episodes. In her longest scene, lasting just over three minutes, she offered Tootie advice about boys. "Let them down softly," she said. "Remember their feelings."

By the time I saw this episode, already in syndication, I was liv-ing with my Aunt Vera, who ironically described herself as the modest underachiever of her family. Instead of following her family into acting, she'd sidestepped the awful parade of callbacks and found work as a stu-dio seamstress, basting skirts and placing darts into dinner jackets for actors who'd lost weight the previous week. I thought of her as an older sister, the role model I lacked in my immediate family.

Even in elementary school, I had a firm understanding of my par-ents. They stood out in such a way that business associates imagined them as more talented, more successful than they actually were. Despite their failures, my parents exuded an aura of achievement. Often they were the objects of social crushes. And the sad part, the tragedy—they passed their gift along to me.

I referred to this element as the "X factor," the reason an averagely talented actor, such as Tom Hanks, was repeatedly nominated for Academy Awards. This explained why one hardworking individual grew up to become studio prop manager, responsible for seven employees, and another equally hardworking man grew up to become Michael Eisner, CEO of Disney.

How I learned to conceal it, my glass heart, this green lantern flashing its code of lies: I wore outdated clothes. I let my hair grow long. I became a stocky adolescent camouflaged inside a thin jacket of fat. At parties I would make a point of greeting only those people I knew. I was careful not to make eye contact too often lest classmates mistakenly glimpse some foreign quality inside me, some element of grace—or, as my aunt explained, the "pixie dust" of celebrity, a chemical that had the ability to turn people like me into people like my parents. My fears were those of most backlot kids. I did not want to become an asshole.

Much to my relief, my parents moved to Manhattan during my senior year of high school, leaving me in my aunt's care. Officially they were moving for "job opportunities"—my mother would sing off-Broadway, my father finance a third Crocodile Dundee movie—but unofficially, they were bored with LA, its new-money clubbiness, its under-thirty mentality. Without them, I thought I'd be able to push beyond the studio gates, but I spent most of my free time with other chubby teenaged children of studio hands and character actors. Occasionally they nudged me in some democratic way toward a position of leadership, but by then I'd learned to exude a mannered slack, to will my eyes toward dullness, thereby confusing people. I sent mixed signals. I wanted nothing more than to sit among my friends as a true equal, sharing family disappointments as well as an occasional joint and predicting which new shows were sure to flop.

Of all my friends, Jenny Rogers seemed to understand me best. Jenny was the daughter of a character actor, the man who had once played Kate Jackson's recurring love interest on *Charlie's Angels*. She was not inflicted with the gift—at least not to the extent I was—and because of this I loved to watch the ways she could appear momentarily unaware. A longtime studio brat, she knew how to look beyond the flashing light of my soul, that shiny bit of phosphorescence other people found so distracting. Not since third grade, when Tommy Morgan had told me that as a shortstop I "sucked the big one," had I felt so understood, so at peace with myself. In subsequent meetings Tommy had told me that my mother's acting ability "blew" and that I'd probably grow up and become a "dickhead." For weeks I longed to be around him, to hear what other insights he might have about my life. At recess I stood in line to challenge him at handball. I arranged my place in the cafeteria line so I'd end up at his table. How I wanted him to like me, to find something of value inside me, because he was not affected by the worthless sheen that attracted the other children.

Perhaps my life might have turned out differently if Tommy had consented to be my friend—if he'd taken a good long look and noticed something, my love of screwball Disney comedies, let's say—but he didn't. A few months after he made that first astute observation, his family moved to Seattle. On the day they left, all of them packed into a Volvo station wagon, I made one last trip to his neighborhood on a Schwinn ten-speed my mother had purchased during one of her periods of compulsive exercise. Leaning against an elm, I saw their car pull up the street much earlier than I'd anticipated. Tommy's parting gesture was a smirk, his upper-lip curled in an expression of sourness, an expression so transparent and belittling that for weeks I walked around school wearing only cheap studio T-shirts, something inside of my tin chest drumming out the message, *love me, love me, love me.* And the horrible part: they did love me, my classmates, in all their unquestioning, un-Tommy-like enthusiasm. They loved me without understanding me, which made me despise whatever strange privilege I'd been given in this world.

In those early weeks I expected to find something similar with

Jenny, some odd mix of chemicals that would allow her to see me as I really was, something of a loser, a boy who got Bs and Cs, so enigmatically injured by his parents that he'd declined to see them over spring break. Rather she saw me as angry—angry because I'd grown up in Santa Monica apartments, because I'd never had close friends, because my parents had moved away for my final year of school. More than once after I'd left her company, I returned to my aunt's trailer, revisiting our conversations. I saw them on an imaginary screen, my lips forming lines of dialogue so accurately that Mr. Forester, manager of the foley shop, once thought I was speaking to him.

Over lentil soup I asked my aunt, "Do you think I'm angry?"

She was an elegant woman, but she dressed in such a way that no actresses her age ever found her beauty a threat. She considered my question, frowning in concentration. "Anger is a difficult phase," she announced, before dipping her spoon into her bowl.

And so, without realizing the consequences of my actions, I began to reconsider my life—to view my past through a different window. During my final month of high school, as my classmates were signing yearbooks and discussing the looming strangeness of college, I was working through my first postadolescent transformation, believing that all along people had been attracted to a latent sense of anger brewing inside me. I saw myself as a descendant of James Dean as he appeared in *Rebel without a Cause:* a loner, pissed off at the fallout of my parents' lives.

As I continued down my path toward anger—or rather toward my acceptance of anger—I spent more time with Jenny. We kissed in wardrobe storage lockers amidst gowns worn by Reese Witherspoon and Sarah Jessica Parker. Surrounded by clothes, we were learning to take ours off, piece by piece, like a drawn-out love sequence in a summer film. We were slow, awkward lovers, unsure of our bodies, and afterward, as we lay half-dressed on the locker floor, we looked up as dust motes swirled in a shaft of afternoon light. She confessed she was angry, too; angry at her father for valuing his career over her, over his first wife, over his second. In such moments, as our souls bent toward confession, I believed that I was growing up, that I was learning to carry myself as an adult.

A few weeks after graduation I took a job—a practical one like my aunt's—as a gaffer's assistant at Studio 5A, which produced regional programming such as *Talk LA, Healthwise,* and *West Coast Review.* Each morning I met Earl, the lighting engineer, who taught me how to set the light grid—the intricate arrangement of semi-diffused spots for *Healthwise* and the low overheads with amber gels for *Talk LA.* Earl was impressed at how quickly I picked up these tasks, the careful way I taped loose cords and secured the backdrop long before the TV "personalities" arrived for makeup.

I enjoyed the work, menial as it was, because it gave me something useful to do after Jenny and I broke up. We separated in part because she was leaving for college but also because I'd come to suspect I wasn't angry, at least not in the sense she'd suggested. Rather anger was at the core of *her* personality. She'd sensed in me a comrade, a studio twin— she'd fallen under the spell of my dreaded gift and convinced herself we were the same. We separated on a Friday night, but for weeks I continued to think about her. Occasionally I visited the locker where we first made love, noting that the gowns had not been moved and that no one had collected the empty soda cup we'd left on the floor.

¤

I had good sense about the studio. I knew how to talk to people, how to play off my lingering sense of anger as an affectation of my youth. Moreover, most studio employees knew how to talk to me. They would tease me, calling me a studio brat or, once, a chubby mama's boy. How I loved their little digs, the suggestion that I had an average soul. Though a few of them were failed actors, most were simple tradesmen with ambitions no larger than to bring home a check each week. Together we went to seedy bars around the airport, where no one checked my ID, to share pitchers of American draft beer and fattening snacks. But even under such auspicious circumstances, I was not one to get drunk; I was afraid I might turn garrulous and inexcusably affable. When asked about my childhood I avoided stories that might link my family to the studio. Instead I highlighted middle-class aspects of my upbringing: my father's failed attempt to change the sparkplugs or the time my mother cooked Thanksgiving dinner with the giblet bags tucked inside the turkey.

At the start of my nineteenth year I began to miss my parents—their guarded expressions of approval, their foolish belief in their unlimited success, even the way my father would look at me in a post-cocktail haze, as though thumbing his mental Rolodex to retrieve my exact name. During the previous year, my mother's off-Broadway show, *Heart Songs*, had closed to mixed reviews, and in a typical fit of luck she'd been picked up as a replacement coanchor for *Good Morning, New England*, a regional cable talk-and-news program. Originally she was signed for a two-month stint, but audience support was so strong she was offered the job permanently.

I supposed I might have limped through life in this manner, acquiring basic electrical skills, pretending I'd grown up in a nonstudio family, if it hadn't been for Ronald Bivvins. Ronald appeared that October, a tall, athletic man with short hair and confused blue eyes, a replacement for Bob "The Boss" Olsen, host of our studio's syndicated show, *Healthwise*. At first glance he looked like many such hosts—well-defined arms, a sinewy neck, a stomach so taut it appeared to be made of plastic—yet he lacked some animating breath that would unify these features. In short, he lacked the X factor.

Perhaps I was the first to notice its absence, so skilled was he in creating its symptoms. From years of practice, or so I imagined, he'd been able to modulate his voice into a slightly deeper register in front of the cameras. While taping he moved with the same confidence I'd seen in my father. He demonstrated various step exercises, along with his aerobically skilled assistants, with an air of deep commitment. His soul was the opposite of mine yet I knew we were alike, two fakes, men trying to swap cards out of the hands fate had dealt us.

Between shows I'd walk by his dressing room, electrical cords coiled around one shoulder, though rarely was I able to see him. He rehearsed everything alone, even the impromptu questions he later delivered to special guests. How strange to find someone so like myself, so troubled by the personality he'd been given. From what little I knew of him, I was able to imagine his childhood: a small-town boy, perhaps from Utah, brought up in a house of religious conservatives, a house without a TV. His mother wore denim dresses, polyester hair scarves, "functional" shoes. At school, he'd been picked last for baseball teams even though he was a natural runner. No one asked him to be class vice president even though he was smarter than most kids at his school.

Around the studio he walked with a stiffness that I initially attributed to overexertion with free weights but later realized was an awkwardness he couldn't disguise offstage. His life was rehearsed, whereas mine was haphazard. In the green room, among the bottles of diet soda and veggie platters, I made many attempts to strike up conversation, claiming he was a significant improvement over Bob "The Boss" Olsen and that the exercise segments on *Healthwise* now had the precision they'd always needed. He was gracious in such a distant way I knew my remarks had little effect on him. I might have found his dismissal more disturbing if it wasn't for his preoccupation: his show's ratings were in the toilet.

Twice a week he arrived at Studio 5A, already dressed in his first workout T-shirt and black Lycra leggings. He was amazingly disciplined in the way he reviewed each show's schedule before pumping a little pre-camera iron. Despite his starchy personality, he was extremely well connected. Through friends or friends-of-friends, he'd managed to frequent a number of studio parties, most of which were hosted at homes or private clubs. Because of this, he was able to expand his show's guest list with a little star power. On the day Jane Krakowski of *Ally McBeal* arrived to tape an exercise segment, she seemed more than a little surprised to learn that Ronald was the show's host, not a production assistant.

In the usual course of studio politics, a personality such as Ronald would be slowly removed from social circles, as was the case with Shannen Doherty and Paul Rubens, but in a rare show of support, the staff of *Healthwise* rallied. They acquired a new kitchen set and even found the money to hire three more assistants, believing the show would come off better if Ronald were mixed in with a larger cast. They scheduled short "exercise tours" for him, lining up workout appearances at malls in such aerobically disinclined cities as Houston, Detroit, and Indianapolis. Each event was compressed into a "travel segment" to give viewers the impression that Ronald's popularity was growing. The show's ratings continued to fall, but to everyone's credit, the ratings fell at a much slower rate.

Following the exercise tours, the producers flew in loyal viewers who had slimmed down. Each was advised not to mention Bob "The Boss" Olsen even if he had been the driving force behind their weight loss. When this didn't work, the producers turned to the crew and suggested a select group of us—say, five or six—appear in a weekly segment called "Shaping Up with the Crew" in which we'd talk about our efforts to either lose weight or tone up. A memo attached to our timecards reminded us, "Selected individuals must be committed to physical self-improvement under the guidance of Ronald Bivvins of *Healthwise,* as this segment seeks to showcase personal improvement."

For days I considered putting in my name, laboring under the belief that in such a small role I'd be as invisible as a movie extra. I told myself I'd receive many health-related benefits, but I knew my motivation. I wanted Ronald to notice me, to recognize that we were alike in some important way. With this in mind, I pretended to let my coworkers persuade me.

We taped five shows over two days, thereby limiting set change time. I sat with the other crew members in metal chairs arranged in the side studio. There were five of us: Katrina from wardrobe; Sam the audio man; Beth, an accountant; and Donya, a producer's niece. In front of the cameras, I explained I'd grown up in the Valley (true), that my parents were often away from home (also true), and that before I realized it I'd developed poor eating habits (somewhat true). I said I'd been inspired by Ronald, particularly by his caring attitude. I waited as he offered a practiced nod. I nodded back, and there was beautiful symmetry in this gesture that suggested we'd connected, if only briefly.

At first I followed Ronald's meal plan—chicken and broccoli, low-salt soup and salad—but after talking with my mom, I learned how to supercharge my diet. She taught me little ways to skip meals ("Have a large glass of lemonade") and how to pretend to eat around friends ("At a party, carry a small plate of hors d'oeuvres but never touch them"). Everyone encouraged me, particularly the producers, who gave me one hour off each afternoon to use a treadmill in the executive gym.

On the days Ronald was at the studio I did my best to dress thin, to find just the right clothes to suggest his encouragement was not lost on me. I made sure to drop by the green room between takes; I offered lighting suggestions to improve his "Health Step" segment; I attempted to share little pieces of my life, such as how I'd stopped going to bars with the other crew members. When these didn't produce the intended effect, I made up stories about women who'd turned me down for dates. But he continued to treat me as one of the crew, slapping me on the shoulder, doling out little tips, such as "Remember to drink plenty of water."

During the segments themselves, I never spoke out of turn. I stayed quiet, hoping to minimize the X factor. Still the camera found me, zooming in while other crew members talked, finding angles to suggest I'd lost the most weight, even though I was third overall, behind Beth, who'd started out at 320 pounds, and Sam, whose natural metabolism kicked in once he cut out beer. As we viewed final cuts, I often stood near Ronald, his body damp and tired, hoping we might strike up a conversation. If that didn't work, I followed him to the mailroom so he might see the few pieces of fan mail I'd begun to receive.

Slowly he noticed me, how I was around him slightly more than necessary. I was fascinated by the awkwardness in his natural walk, by the way he liked to have something in his hands at all times, a clipboard, a bottle of purified water. I recognized his vague attempts to flirt with the production staff, women who appeared confused by his interest. With other crew members he tried to be social, telling jokes, but around me he was quiet, though I did my best to draw him out. I asked about his childhood (Oregon, not Utah), about his mother (school accountant), about his interest in exercise (he was good at it). During our short exchanges, he gradually took a mean-spirited delight in ignoring me.

I can't say when I first understood this—the morning he walked away while I was still talking or the afternoon he suggested I redo all the lighting cues—but eventually I sensed that he knew I was a fraud. As we taped our crew segment, he blocked me from the camera. When I stood near him, he moved away. In short conversations he dropped the names of famous people my parents knew. He seemed intent on presenting himself as a Burbank insider, though when I asked my mother, she'd never heard of him.

"Bivvins," she said over the phone. "I knew a Steve Bivvins once."

But the diet was going well. By the end of the sixth week I'd lost twenty-five pounds and was fitting nicely into size thirty-four pants, though I yearned to be a thirty-two as that was my father's size, ideal for a man of my height and build. I did my best to eat very little, to drink eight glasses of water a day, not to step on the scale more than once a week. But rarely did I achieve the ideal life of a *Healthwise* dieter. Some days I fasted until dinner, only to scarf down two handfuls of Doritos. Seldom did I drink my daily allowance of water, but I could suck on diet sodas from dawn until dusk. As for the scale, I shouldn't even tell you my compulsions. Still the weight fell off at the unhealthful but visually impressive rate of four pounds a week.

For the cameras, I talked about a well-rounded meal plan—that is, when Ronald allowed me to talk—naming many of Bivvins's specialty dishes, such as Chicken Orlando and No-Meat Tacos. I even went so far as to suggest supplemental ingredients, such as finely chopped cilantro, that made my stories not only more interesting but more believable. More than once I received little notes from home viewers thanking me: "Banana peppers really livened up the meal!" But Ronald was not fooled. He saw how easily I moved about the studio, how much the crew liked me even though I no longer gave my full attention to gaffing. Once I caught him staring at me as I was changing gels. His expression held a visible confusion that deepened to anger just before he walked away.

On the day I reached my goal weight, Ronald let me sit in the middle of the group. For weeks, I'd felt the other dieters pushing me toward that seat, leaving it open when I arrived last, but Ronald always found some excuse to reseat me. For four minutes straight, I talked about my favorite Bivvins meals, meals that for the most part I'd never even tried to prepare, but I did so in a conscientious way. I discussed those I thought would taste best, such as Spicy Fish Kabobs and Apple-Me-Tenders.

On stage he smiled, but outside the green room, when I was alone, he approached confused and disoriented. He allowed me to stand next to him, a brief moment of silence in which I felt the sheer energy that came from being with my opposite, matter and antimatter.

"You never made Apple-Me-Tenders," he said.

"Yes," I admitted, "but they look very good. I'd like to try them."

"You're a terrible dieter. You're unhealthful."

"That's true," I said encouragingly. "I have trouble with discipline."

He absorbed this information slowly, taking it in the way one might a bad scent. "But everyone likes you."

"They don't really know *me*. You're one of the few people who understand."

He walked away, holding a bottle of purified water, and headed toward the production booth where, the following afternoon we'd learn his show would soon be canceled.

¤

In those final days before production ceased, he didn't work at Studio 5A so much as haunt it. Twice he wore the same red muscle shirt, even though he was supposed to change clothes between shows. No longer did he pump pre-camera iron. He took up the strange habit of whistling the theme song for *Healthwise* in his dressing room. When I asked if he'd attended any good parties, he said, "Plenty," in such a way I knew he'd done little with his free time except stay home and visit the gym.

I felt sorry for him. In the hallway, I complimented him on his lovely stage voice and the heightened sense of rhythm he brought to the step aerobic segments. I thought that with a little encouragement he might better mimic the symptoms of stardom. Yet he ignored my comments, treating me with an indignity so strong I had to leave "anonymous" notes advising him to take one of three agents my mother recommended.

How I wanted him to like me—to tell me that I was a man with no talent, no true work ethic, and then, in the next breath, confess he was drawn to me anyway. But rarely did I see him, let alone talk to him. He spent his time arranging a position as personal trainer to the stars while I went about my tasks, half-heartedly testing spots and reprogramming the light board. I passed into a dark mood, an emptiness I'd not experienced before, so that dieting became easy. I stopped thinking of food and was not tempted by the Doritos I used to enjoy at home.

I did my best to play my moodiness off as a side-effect of my diet, but already crew members were beginning to treat me differently. Earl was happy to redo my gaffing errors, relaying cables, refocusing lights, and the production staff suggested I seek a position in management despite my obvious lack of organization and poor professional demeanor. Without my fat, I was exposed, vulnerable, unable to adequately conceal the terrible gift I'd pushed aside for so many years.

On the day Ronald left for good, I arrived late, as was becoming my habit, and stood with the crew as he packed the last of his personal wardrobe into his car. He moved with a new stiffness others would interpret as resolve but I understood as the lovely mechanism of his body. He shook hands with the production staff but did not face the crew. From his car, he offered us a farewell wave, his eyes lingering on mine. Already I could sense the strange shape of my future. But on that day I simply watched as his car pulled beneath the gilded studio arch, still believing we'd meet again, that he'd like me even though he could see the petty emptiness hidden deep inside my heart.

Day of the Dead

I suppose I should start with Mary. Mary Collier, who worked in the college bookstore. Mary with the lovely brown eyes. I met her the year after my parents died. I was twenty-eight and living under the belief that I was about to turn a corner and start my life over as an adult. But I never seemed to find that corner, nor was I able to shake the feeling of aloneness I felt in the world. Though I'd grown up in California, I was now living in Florida, the panhandle, to be exact. And this is where Mary comes in.

I'd seen her before Henry's party, but that night, while I loaded a paper plate with carrot sticks and celery, I was taken with her, how she stood across the buffet table, her red hair neatly clipped at her shoulders, her inebriate's eyes regarding me with warm indifference. I'd heard stories about her, that she'd stopped dating college faculty, even young, untenured delinquents like me, but later that night, while sitting outside on an Adirondack chair, under a sky hazy with stars, I found her beside me, her eyes a little bleary, her glass half filled with scotch. We talked for a while, mainly about our old dreams: I'd once wanted to be a writer, she a design specialist in New York. When we left the party I was surprised to find we were leaving together, her jacket folded over my arm. She told me she used to be married. "For about three months, until I figured out dear old Rich was really dealing coke on the side." She turned to me. "You ever been married?"

"No."

"Ever come close?"

"I know I'm supposed to say, 'yes,' but the truth is, not really. Grad school doesn't promote marriage."

"I see," she said.

We walked to her condo. Once there, I offered her her coat, only to find that beneath it my hand still clutched a tumbler from the party. "I bet you have a whole mismatched collection of these at home," she teased. I laughed because in part she was right. I did have two glasses I couldn't account for in my cupboard. When we grew quiet again, I thought I'd be dismissed with a smile or a drunken kiss, but to my surprise, she took the tumbler and ran her thumb around its rim. "I could refill this inside," she offered.

Inside I was nervous, though luckily a little drunk as well. Her living room had been converted to a studio, its floor protected by a white tarp. In the center stood two easels, both holding half-finished canvases, realistic reproductions of the Gulf. In the kitchen she uncapped a bottle of gin and refilled my glass, then asked if I wanted ice. "It's fine like this," I said. I leaned against the counter, standing beneath her hand-hammered copper pots, my feet crossed at the ankles. After she'd taken a drink, I put my hand on her hip, tentatively. Her body offered the slightest acquiescence as she tilted her head toward mine.

I kissed her, wide-mouthed and eager. "I'm really drunk," I said. "Finish your gin," she said.

Already I was falling for her. Our lips touched, and she hooked her thumbs under my belt. Carefully I maneuvered her against the counter, beside the blender and coffeemaker. Once I regained full balance, I unbuttoned her sweater, revealing her stomach, complete with a silver bellybutton ring. When I reached the fourth button, the one that, when released, would allow her breasts, unhampered by a bra, to spill into my hands, she stopped me, her fingers gently cuffed around my wrists. I wondered if at this late hour, I would be ushered to the door, another spurned suitor. She placed my hands on the counter. "If you keep them there," she said, "I'll keep going."

In a motion I can best describe as defiant, she stepped into the center of her kitchen, where moonlight slanted in around her, and unzipped her skirt, allowing it to fall like a shadow around her feet. She worked her black panties down her legs, revealing a smudge of auburn pubic hair. "You could touch me," she teased, "but of course then I'd have to stop."

"Of course," I repeated. Though I suspected she might *not* actually stop, I stayed put, my hands clamped to the counter. I'd slept with a few women in college, a few more in grad school, but never anyone like Mary. I felt lucky to be there, lucky because she understood the world in a way I did not. She allowed me to look until an erection pushed against the cheap khaki fabric of my chinos. She traced its outline with two fingers. Only then did she undo the final button of her sweater, allowing the halves to part like a theater curtain and reveal the clean curve of her breasts.

"I always like to hold something back," she said, "until I know where I stand."

I wanted to say something witty but couldn't think of anything, so

I simply kissed her, my arms circled around her bare back. "Move your hands a little higher," she suggested, then we began to kiss again.

¤

As you can probably guess, I fell for her in the worst way. I found reasons to go by the bookstore around closing time. I let my junior American Lit class out early so I might see her on the library green, where she often ate lunch with other people from work. The week before her twenty-sixth birthday, I called my credit card company to see if I had enough available credit to buy her a strand of pearls. I did.

Though I knew she was out of my league, I kept going over to her house, kept buying her little gifts such as flowers and perfume. She liked to make love with me because she was better at it than I was, but I didn't care. I was delighted that she was sleeping with me, delighted I no longer had to lie in my own full-size bed alone, bundled under a thin nylon comforter as car lights moved across my window. While I dated her, I lapsed into a grad school fascination with sex, a hazy sense that it would teach me something important about myself, something that I should have learned years ago.

In the mornings she looked so pretty, pillow lines gracing her cheek. Every now and then she glanced over my class handouts in such a way I thought she was impressed. Around campus I felt confident, full of dreamy good will and generosity. I saw us as the artist and the teacher, people naturally drawn together. I told myself Mary valued things in me I couldn't yet see, qualities that might keep us together. For our five-month anniversary, I took her to the best seafood restaurant on the Gulf. Then it happened:

She dumped me on a bright July day, right after I'd finished teaching remedial composition to hulking football players who couldn't operate a Speak & Spell, let alone write a term paper. After I left her condo, my toothbrush and aftershave stowed in a Nine West shoebox, I sat on her steps long enough to meet the florist who was delivering a half-dozen long stems packed into a clear, plastic box. The envelope simply read "To M—", and I wondered who in the world could possibly know her well enough to address her as M—.

Following this, many male colleagues happened to show up at my office, some of them too tickled not to grin. They asked me how the teaching was going, if I wanted to grab a drink after work, but what they really wanted was to see me cut down to size, sad and lonely, unshaven, too despondent to wear anything but shorts and T-shirts. My only friend during the whole ordeal was Henry, at whose party I'd met Mary. He taught history and, like me, was young and untenured. He was a quiet, respectable person, who favored oxford shirts and chinos. He was a good listener and, despite the fact that he was easy-going and good-looking, he hadn't dated many women since graduate school either. On weekends we drank at his house. When I was sufficiently drunk I wanted to tell him how much I missed Mary, but instead I told him about various sex games we'd played, one in particular that involved massage oil, large black trash bags and strips of fabric cut to one-foot lengths. "Did she really say, 'Don't move your hands?'" he asked.

"It wasn't even a date," I explained. "It was like a pre-date. It happened the night of your party."

Without a doubt, he was a good friend to me. He let me sleep on his couch when I was too far gone to make it home; he rolled his eyes when I read excerpts from papers students had gratuitously plagiarized; most importantly, he let me think my experience with Mary was important and useful and that I was not stupid, stupid, stupid for dating her in the first place.

In the weeks that followed our breakup, I drove by her condo at night, noting the red Honda Accord often parked in her visitor's space. I continued to see her at the bookstore, even though I went there only to place text orders and to pick up books I'd requested earlier that year.

She'd lost weight and begun to wear long, elegant dresses that I'm certain she didn't own while we were dating. She'd let her hair grow long and, toward the end of August, had it highlighted. She looked so pretty my heart hurt every time I saw her. Except for one desperate late-night phone call, I never again broke down and told her how much I loved her and that I had been a better person while in her presence. Instead, I let myself fall out of love and into a pit so dimly lit that once, while teaching my junior lit seminar, I suggested the tragic romance in *Madame Bovary* might have been intended as highbrow comedy or even as farce. My best students looked at me as though I were stark raving mad. The others faithfully copied this idea into their spiral notebooks just in case it showed up on the final.

The one irony of the story is this: during that summer when I missed Mary so much I lost fifteen pounds and slept less than certain species of carpenter ants, my friend Henry was falling in love for the first time in years. At a conference on the Religious History of the South, he'd met a woman named Sarah Simms, who held a temporary research appointment at Tulane University. By August he was making twice-monthly trips to New Orleans, and by September he was going every week.

In mid-October, Sarah finally spent the weekend with him in Florida. She had a warm, genuine personality and, like most university women I'd met, made direct eye contact with the men in the room as a way of asserting her equality. She wore a sundress, sandals, and a necklace made of polished stones. At our first meeting, a Friday gathering at Henry's, she told me she was researching the intersection between Creole beliefs and the religious customs brought to America by African slaves. She had studied other religious interchanges and had an NEH grant to study the influence of Wesley later that year. I was impressed because she was not quite the person I thought she'd be. She was confident, smart, and beautiful, and as far as I could tell, liked Henry as much as he liked her. They spent the rest of the weekend by themselves, except for brunch on Sunday.

Talking to me alone, she said, "Because of you, Henry keeps suggesting we do something with Hefty bags."

"It's not as strange as you think," I said.

"I keep telling him I'm game, but he never follows through." She touched my elbow and moved beside me. "I hear you're single at the moment."

"You hear right."

"I have some friends. I could fix you up."

"To be honest," I said, "this last go-round didn't end well. I don't think I'm up for it yet."

"Still, if you change your mind, let me know."

At the table she sat next to Henry, her hand on his knee. They looked good together, the worldly history professor and the earthy researcher. While I was with them I felt a hole open inside of me, a deep empty place I didn't like to think was there. I wanted to be happy, like Henry was happy, though I suspected I wouldn't date anyone for a long time.

For the first two days of her visit, I saw them as an ideal couple, two people destined to be together, but on that Sunday, when Henry was in the men's room, she spoke to our waiter, whom, coincidentally, she knew from New Orleans. I was not close enough to hear their exchange, but as she spoke she smiled flirtatiously, adopted a coy stance, and ran her fingers through her hair. She placed her hand on his shoulder, letting it linger too long to be a purely platonic gesture. When Henry emerged, she arranged herself as the person she'd been earlier that day. Holding hands, she and Henry made their way around the buffet table to meet us outside.

The following day Henry asked what I thought of her. We were sitting at Jack's Bar, finishing off some hot wings and beer. "I like her," I said. "She's pretty and has a nice personality."

"But?" he said. "With you there's always a *but*."

"There's not always a *but*," I said. I set my mug on the table. "*But* she's going to break your heart."

"You're always down on romance. Just because your relationship with Mary was doomed, you think all relationships will work out that way."

"It's just a feeling," I said.

He signaled the waitress for two more Coronas. "She's having a Halloween party," he said. "I want you to go."

"To the French Quarter? It'll be a zoo."

"She lives in a nice part of the Quarter. It'll be a quiet, private party. Besides it'll do you a world of good to get out of this dumpy town for a day or two."

"Day *or two*?" I said. "How long does this party last?"

"One night. You can stay at her house. She has an extra room."

The waitress delivered our beers, then left.

"Let me think about it," I said. "I don't know if I'm up for the French Quarter on Halloween. I mean, my trauma card's pretty much filled for the year."

He touched his beer to mine. "I'm leaving Saturday afternoon," he said.

☿

Though I tactfully tried to get out of going, I felt obligated each time Henry brought it up—so much so that I found myself in his aqua blue Taurus that Saturday, driving west. He was dressed as a priest, complete with collar and thin gold cross, whereas I was simply dressed as my-self, white shirt and khakis, penny loafers on my feet. After we'd driven through the Mobile Tunnel, he set the cruise control at seventy, turned to me, and asked why I was not wearing a costume.

"To be honest, Henry, I figured I'd be able to weasel out at the last minute. I know it's a party. I know I'm supposed to have fun. But I have this bad feeling I'll be nothing more than a third wheel all weekend."

"You won't be a third wheel," he said. "There'll be a lot of people there. Really, you'll have a good time." We passed a tanker marked "Danger: Explosives" then pulled into open road. Outside, swamp pines lined the freeway; above us clouds striped the sky. "You want to stop and get a costume?" he offered. "My treat."

"If people ask, say I *am* wearing a costume." I turned to Henry. His eyes appeared sad. "Tell them I'm going as a Party Pooper. They'll think that's funny."

"You know," he said, "that *is* kind of funny."

We made good time across Alabama and Mississippi, stopping only once to buy gas. I began to sense that Henry was upset—he was quiet and kept fiddling with the radio—and because I am self-centered at times, I figured this was probably my fault, because I'd tried to get out of going, though clearly I owed him more favors than the people of Kuwait collectively owed the United Nations. I saw myself as this small, selfish person unwilling to accompany his best friend to a Halloween party, a person who would only go grumbling, and with no costume to boot.

As we pulled across the Louisiana state border, I tried to make small talk. He said the party was an annual event put on by the person who held the Visiting Research Chair, i.e., Sarah, even though her term would soon expire. While driving over Lake Pontchartrain, he checked his priest's collar three times, centering the white square directly below his Adam's apple, and then, after switching the radio off, he looked at me, his face a mixture of anxiety and lost hope.

"Okay," I finally said, "I'm sorry I didn't wear a costume. I know I haven't been a very good friend. If you stop at a store I'll buy one, no matter what the cost."

"No," he said, "you're going as a Party Pooper. You'll be more comfortable that way. I realize you didn't want to go. I was asking a lot."

By now we were in New Orleans, the skyline of downtown directly ahead of us, charcoal and modern, silhouetted against a twilight sky. Unlike the cities of my childhood, New Orleans built its freeways above existing neighborhoods, an elaborate system of cement crisscrossing the sky, touching down, then rising up like an elongated row of Ms. We were on the bridge that would take us to the French Quarter, the Vieux Carré, and just as we were lifting onto another incline, Henry reached into his priest's jacket and withdrew a small packaged wrapped in a handkerchief and tied in a hobo's knot. "Open it," he said.

I undid the knot and found a smooth turquoise stone slightly smaller than a golf ball beside a white envelope. I held the stone, testing its weight. "What's this?" I asked.

"Sarah gave it to me," he said. "It was blessed by a tribe elder out in New Mexico. It's supposed to bring you good luck."

I looked at the stone, then at Henry. Even though he was pushing seventy-five on one of the worst-maintained freeways in America, he was checking his collar one last time. "Did you and Sarah have a fight?"

"Open the envelope," he said.

Nestled inside the envelope was a ring—clearly an engagement ring, a large solitaire attached to a gold band. Though I'm not an expert on diamonds, I believe it was a princess cut, much larger than he could afford. Henry was still tinkering with his damn collar. Only then did I understand how much he loved her, how desperate he was, how nervous.

"She's not going to say yes," he said.

"Of course she is. You don't know that."

"She's leaving in a month. I want to do this tonight. You're here to drive me home after it all falls apart." I handed him the package, which he refused by waving his hand. "Give it to me later," he said, "when I ask for it."

I turned to him, my best friend, my anxious priest. Though I was soon to be listed in the *Guinness Book of Third Wheels* under the heading "Man Accompanies Friend on Engagement Date," I felt more sorry for him than I had for anyone in years. He was the most vulnerable of men, a lovesick academic who wore his heart on his sleeve. From experience, I'd learned academics are not good at sensing their blind spots, nor are they good at managing emotions. For the most part they've been trained to be straightforward truth tellers, even when the truth will do them more harm than good. "Know this," I said. "She'll never find anyone better than you. She'd be a fool to turn you down."

"I know," he said, "but doubt it will do me much good tonight."

¤

As expected, we couldn't park anywhere near the actual party—her street was lined with cars—so we parked in a public lot three blocks away. Already the French Quarter was packed with people, most of them college students stumbling around with beer or frozen drinks. While walking to Sarah's house we passed groups of gay men dressed as David statues, their bodies dusted with talcum. At the corner of Urseline and Bourbon, I forced Henry into a bar. We walked past a sign that read "Day of the Dead—All Welcome," then another that requested we "Remove All Halloween Masks before Entering." Inside, we found more gay men, most dressed in leather, one of whom looked like the S&M version of Pinocchio. At the bar I ordered two shots of Jack. The bartender, dressed in drag, said, "You're the only person here not in fancy dress."

"But he is," Henry offered. "He's a Party Pooper."

The bartender squinted at me, his pancake base cracking around his mouth. "I'm glad he's not my date, Father. It's a bad night for party poopers here in the Quarter."

By the time we arrived at the party I was feeling better, that is, I had a little buzz going. Sarah met us at the door, dressed as a nun, and ushered us in. "Very cute," I said, "matching costumes."

"We arranged it last week," she explained.

"If I would've known, I could've come as an altar boy."

"He's a Party Pooper," Henry said.

Sarah scowled at him.

"He means, it's my costume," I explained.

She guided us through the house, pointing out a few architectural points of interest, though for the most part, hers was like most French American cottages in the Quarter: solid wood floors, high ceilings, decorative ironwork doors leading to a hidden courtyard where a naked prepubescent angel held a potted fern above his head while peeing continuously into a fountain. I was surprised how many people knew Henry. He had a larger social life here than he'd ever had in Florida. I was surprised, too, that Sarah had cut her hair and, in an odd way, reminded me of Mary. The way she walked and looked at people suggested she was happy with her single life, perhaps unwilling to have attachments more serious than a boyfriend. "Look," I said after she completed the tour, "you don't want me hanging around you all night. Why don't you two say hello to each other. I'm going to fix myself a drink."

I made my way to the bar and did my best to mix in. Her house was filled with at least fifty people, most in costume. Three women were dressed as dark angels, their bodies covered simply by black leotards and wings. One man came as Bill Clinton, his boxers hanging out of his fly. There were the usual women as black cats, men as devils, but by far the most popular costume was lingerie. While standing at the bar I counted seven women who wore lingerie as their costume, the prettiest modeled a white silk teddy and opaque leggings.

I searched for my old standby, but finding no gin I made a Jack and Coke. While I was recapping the bottle, a woman dressed as a French maid asked me for a tequila sunrise. I did my best, going heavy on the alcohol. When I handed it to her, she winked at me. "This party's got a nice atmosphere," she said. "It's all kind of sexy." Then she walked away to join her companion, dressed as Adam, an apple in one hand, a long stretch of brown fabric covering his groin.

I was doing my best to get with the crowd, join the party. I found that the French maid had been right, there was something sensuous here that even I could not ignore. By now most of the faculty had left, or at least had withdrawn to the courtyard. The stereo pumped out an odd mix of blues interspersed with Michael Jackson's *Thriller*. I was over by the buffet table when I noticed one of my own students, Julie Newman, wearing a cocktail dress and heels. She was with two other girls, one of whom wore a black lace bra and mini-skirt. I was unsure if this was a costume or not. "Professor Bryce," she yelled, "what're you doing here?" She turned to her friends. "This is my English teacher, from Florida."

They stopped to check me out. Unimpressed, they turned away.

"My best friend goes to Tulane," she explained. "What a trip finding you here! You're so different in class."

"It's all smoke and mirrors," I said.

"We're going to check out Bourbon Street later. How about you?"

"Not me. I'm on damage control. My best friend's in love with the woman giving this shindig."

"The Nun?" she asked. "She's cool. She flashed us earlier. Under her habit she's wearing leather and lace. I mean, the Madonna and whore all in one."

"I didn't know that," I said.

"It's such an outrageous costume. Two opposites together, you

know, like how *Madame Bovary* is tragedy and a comedy all at once."
She smiled at me. "But I still haven't got to the funny parts yet."

At about this time, I noticed that one of the lingerie girls was look-ing at me, the one I'd noticed earlier, wearing the white silk teddy and opaque leggings. She stood near the stereo, sipping her drink through a straw. Unlike the other lingerie girls, she looked somewhat shy and self-conscious, checking her costume every minute or two to make sure it didn't reveal too much. "Did you say your name was Bryce?" she asked when I finally met her. She stood beside me, her drink mostly finished, her arms close to her body.

"Yeah, I'm Bryce," I said.

"You're Henry's friend, right? I've heard about you."

"Apparently everyone has—the thing with the trash bags, right?"

"No," she said, "that you teach in Florida. What's the thing with the trash bags?"

"Nothing," I said. "Forget it."

She told me that her name was Melanie and that she was a grad student at Tulane. "Some party. How come you're not in costume?"

"Long story."

"I've always wanted to wear a teddy to a party but now I feel kind of foolish. It's not me at all."

"You don't look foolish," I said. "You look very nice."

At this she softened. She looked at me differently, her eyes wide, her arms falling more naturally at her sides, and in that moment, she sized me up and made some decisions about me. Though I do not know what those were, I must've fared well in the analysis because she touched her glass to mine, a mock toast. "Have you been to the Quarter for Hal-loween before?"

"No," I said.

"You should go up to Bourbon Street."

"I'm not sure that's on the agenda."

"It could be," she said, "later."

Shortly after this we separated, she going back to her friends, me going off to the buffet table, though I noticed that she checked to see where I was going, her deep brown eyes moving across the room before alighting on me, but of course by saying that I'm admitting that I was looking at her as well. I liked how she stood with her girlfriends—a black cat, an angel, and a pirate wench—though clearly she was a little nervous to be wearing nothing more than lingerie. At the buffet table I loaded a plate with two dinner rolls and some sliced Swiss cheese.

Henry and Sarah for the most part stayed in the courtyard, where moonlight angled in around them and where someone (probably Sarah) had fired up the tiki torches. They stood near the naked angel boy, talking to her friends. When I came outside, drink in hand, they seemed not to notice me. Sarah was a tall, gregarious woman, a person hooked on research in a way I'd never been. She had a natural flirtatiousness about her, a certain charm men found endearing. She was talking to a group of professors but when she returned to Henry, she did something that surprised me: she looped her rosary beads around his neck so they were lassoed together, ordained members of the Catholic Church taking a walk on the wild side. For the first time, I saw that maybe she would say yes, that perhaps I'd read the situation wrong, though I did not know if this was a true impression or not.

"So," I said, when Sarah came over to see me, "I hear you're an entirely different person under that habit."

"I hear *you've* been flirting with Melanie."

"We've talked," I said. Sarah stood beside me. Together, we surveyed the party. A man wearing a horned Viking helmet stood in the fountain. Beside him, a man in women's undergarments posed beside the angel statue to have his photo taken. "Tell me something," I said, "do you love Henry?"

"You're a good friend to ask."

"I don't know if I'd say that," I said.

"I have a feeling where this night's going to end up. Henry says he needs to get a package from you."

"I have that package," I said. "So when all is said and done, will this night turn out how he wants it to?"

"I'm not sure," she said, "I need to talk to him about a few things. It could end up there. I wouldn't be an easy person to live with. I'm a researcher. I travel a lot."

"Henry understands that," I said. "I think it'll be okay."

"I hope so," she said, "but I need to hear it from him. For a researcher, I'm a very intuitive person. I need to feel right about something before I do it."

"Do you have that right feeling?"

"Not yet," she said, "but I'm moving in that direction."

"Moving," I said, "is good."

After Sarah was called away—something about people having sex in her shower—Henry came over, his priest's collar undone, his hair unkempt and knotted. He was nervous but doing his best to appear like one cool customer. "Got the ring?" he asked.

"I've got it," I said. I looked at it one last time, nestled in the handkerchief, before handing it to him. "You're one lucky man if she has you. She's a good woman."

"Think she'll say yes?"

"She's leaning that way. She has some minor reservations, but overall I feel good about it."

"I feel good too," he said. He undid the handkerchief then pressed his good luck stone into my palm.

"Don't you want this?"

"You keep it," he said. "Did I ever tell you I asked a woman when I was an undergrad?"

"No," I said.

"I didn't even get the ring out before she said, 'Henry, you can't be serious.'"

"I've got higher hopes for tonight."

"Me, too," he said. "I'm ready to ride it out."

With that he left, ring in pocket, and went to find Sarah. A few minutes later—though I'm not entirely sure about the details—they left the party and walked down to the mighty Mississippi, where he planned to propose. With them gone, I was oddly relegated to the role of party host, all complaints finding their way to me. When the couple returned to the shower, I simply knocked on the door. To the man unzipping in the bushes, I said the bathroom was now available. For the *I Dream of Jeannie* who'd lost her top, I found one of Sarah's T-shirts, asking her to return it later that week.

All in all I did a good job as ad-hoc host. When the party began to wind down, I found Melanie, still in her white teddy, waiting for me on Sarah's couch. Only then did I realize she was somewhat reserved, hoping a party in the French Quarter would help her take hold of some larger, more outgoing personality, and though I didn't know it before I sat next to her, I had similar hopes for my own life as well. Around her, I felt awkward and unsure of myself. "Can I kiss you?" I asked.

"Don't ask," she said, "just kiss me."

I put my arms around her silky waist and slowly brought our lips into a tentative, open-eyed kiss, a union so sweet and hopeful I followed it with another, this one holding a small nugget of passion, my hands up around her rib cage. Her eyes searched me—for what, I don't know— then she rose, her teddy hanging lower than it had earlier that evening, a run traveling the length of her leggings. "Come with me," she said. "I want to see Bourbon Street."

"Are we going to end up at your place?"

"We might."

"I need to leave your number, just in case. Henry hasn't gotten back yet."

"I wish I had friends like you."

"You're just seeing me at a good moment," I said.

¤

Outside, people streamed down the street. We saw men dressed as Vegas showgirls, complete with feather headdresses and heels. We saw groups of tourists in Harlequin masks and two women wearing striped pajamas and slippers. We moved in and out of the crowd, music floating around us, the incense so strong I felt lightheaded. While I bought drinks from a Lucky Dog cart, we saw Henry and Sarah stroll down the street opposite us, their arms tight around each other, clearly engaged. Seeing this, Melanie moved beside me. She curved her hand around mine, then let go.

Once on Bourbon, we were caught up with the college students, a mass of people crawling from bar to bar. Members of New Orleans's finest sat atop horses, a garage band belted out a grunge version of "When the Saints Go Marching In," and homeless street vendors pushed through the mob, hawking roses, hats and T-shirts. Melanie stayed close, her shoulder touching mine, and when the crowd thickened, she took my hand again.

In the street beneath hotel balconies, women lifted their shirts and exposed their breasts in exchange for beads dropped from balconies. Likewise, a few men, wearing shorts or just boxers, waggled their dicks until beads were dropped like plastic manna into their open hands. Countless men with camcorders captured it all on home video.

Surprisingly, I liked being there, my arm around Melanie. I liked, too, the energy swirling around me: I understood I'd been lost for a long time and did not want to be lost anymore. As we passed beneath a hotel balcony, a man dressed as a monk used a laser pointer to draw a luminous red circle around Melanie's breasts. "Stay here," she said, handing her small cocktail purse to me.

Stepping into a clearing, she looked at the monk, who now dangled beads, offering an exchange. They were nice beads, too, much prettier than those other people wore: large purple and green orbs intermixed with red hearts. She looked at me, doing her best to pretend she was a bad girl, though we both knew she was not. By now a small circle had formed around her, men with cameras mainly, and when she lowered her teddy, tugging it down around her stomach, cameras flashed as though she were a movie star and not a graduate student at Tulane University. She looked so beautiful just then, staring at no one but me, her breasts white as cream, ending in pink aureoles. After she'd covered herself, her beads—her beautiful purple and green beads—were dropped from the balcony into her waiting hands.

We were about to leave, my arm around her, when we saw a similar red light on me. Looking up, I saw a woman dressed in a beige body stocking, a strand of beads dangling from her hand. These were not as nice as the beads Melanie had received, though they did have a large blue medallion attached to them. I was ready to move on, but noticed people had formed an arc around me, a number of women, most of them drunk, a few men as well. "Show it," one of them yelled. I looked to Melanie, who stood beside me. Perhaps I was reading her wrong, but I thought I saw encouragement in her eyes, the hope that I'd join her in this night of costumed debauchery. She moved behind me, her arms looped around my waist. While I was considering the proposition, she took my hand and squeezed it.

By now more people had gathered, not so much to see what I might show but because I was hesitant and having second thoughts. They wanted to see if I would do this or not. More specifically, they wanted to see if a good dose of peer pressure would push me over the edge. I was losing myself into the crowd, Melanie behind me, the beads above, a group of drunk people cheering me on. "The big D," one of them yelled. "Let's see it."

"Show us the big D," another cried.

People pressed in, women with cameras. One let out a long, loud wolf whistle. When I began to unfasten my belt they cheered. I wanted to be with Melanie, to join her in this place. I undid my pants and when I had my shorts down, my dick dangling like a dowsing rod, cameras flashing like hell—only then did I see my student, Julie Newman, standing at the front of the crowd, yelling and dancing, her hands above her head. Clearly she was drunk, moved by the crowd as much as I was. "Woo-hoo, Professor Bryce," she yelled, "you go for it. Wave that thing." I looked at her, gyrating away, shock and horror mapped across my face. Melanie noticed the change in me: her gaze shifted from me to Julie, then to me again. "A student," I mouthed, and for a moment, I forgot where I was. I looked up just in time to see my beads, weighted by a large medallion, fall from the balcony. They fell much faster than I'd expected, hurtling through the darkness, and struck me full force in the eye. The crowd twisted itself into iridescent slits, and I felt two thumps against my back.

Though I'm not positive, I believe I lost consciousness for a moment. When I regained a sense of myself I was sitting on the street, my moment in the spotlight having ended. At first I was unsure where I was, but then saw Melanie, her white teddy now splashed with beer. She helped me to my feet and handed me my beads. She seemed to be reconsidering this night.

She moved beside me, her eyes studying mine. Did she understand that I was a lost, wandering man, a man who was not good at love, though he wanted to be, a man who pretended to be more confident than he felt? She crossed her arms then uncrossed them. I was about to explain, but her features softened. We stood on Bourbon Street as people pushed past us. A brass band played in the distance. Cheap roadside fireworks blossomed overhead. "Come on," she finally whispered. "Follow me home."

The Real World

I

For a couple of weeks we had peace, more peace than you'd expect here at *The Real World* house, New Orleans. The reason for this peace was that my boyfriend found out his mother had breast cancer, a small lump under her left armpit. Malignant, she told him over the phone. Shortly after their conversation ended, our segment director, Sanchez, emerged from the basement control room, along with a cameraman and a sound guy. He stood in the kitchen, confused, and ran his hands through his short, black hair. "Listen, Jason," he said, "I've never made this offer to anyone. But we don't need to use this if you don't want us to."

"No," Jason said, "I'm cool with whatever."

For the rest of the evening, Jason hung out by our front gate, his smoky eyes gazing off at the horizon. We lived in a Garden District

Victorian, complete with a security entrance and turn-of-the-century wooden gazebo. He leaned against a tree, his arms crossed in such a way that his biceps tightened into visible knots, while Sanchez filmed him through a second-story window. Occasionally kids would drive by and yell things like "*The Real World* is for losers," but by now we were good at ignoring these insults.

That night I returned with my roommate, Brandy, after dark. I'd gone to an AA meeting with her because during our second month in New Orleans she'd partied with these frat guys then turned up in the ER with her blood-alcohol level at .27. "Thing I like most about those AA meetings," she said, "no cameras. They just don't put up with shit like that."

"Sanchez films you walking in and out of that place every other week."

"Still, he can't go in. Those AA people make me turn off my mike, too." She tapped her chest twice, right where Sandy, the production assistant, had wired her that morning. "You have to respect your fellow alkies."

We stopped a block from the house so Brandy could check her lipstick. I'd never seen a girl who could apply lipstick as perfectly as Brandy. She was from South Central; I from up north. After dinner we had a full night lined up. We were required to attend an HIV fundraiser as part of our *RW* community service project, and later we were going to check out the bands up on Bourbon. Brandy had been to AA before and was already accustomed to sipping diet Cokes at bars.

At first we didn't notice anything different about the house, except that the lights were still on day mode—the crew controls the lights to optimize filming—but as we walked through the living room, we saw Janice in the hot tub wearing her bikini, her arms folded beneath her breasts. Janice hadn't worn her bikini since Week Two, when bad boy

Isaac had talked her into playing Truth or Dare while the crew from *Road Rules* was visiting us.

I found Jason in my bedroom, a washcloth folded over his eyes, the curtains shut. Already, he'd placed my Gap nightshirt over the in-room camera, a lipstick unit hidden between my John Irving novels and a Trivial Pursuit box. He sat up long enough to tell me about his mom. "They're going to take it out in a couple weeks," he said. Though he tried to sound optimistic, I noticed how his gaze kept shifting away from me.

Downstairs, I told Brandy I was going to blow off the HIV fundraiser. "Jason's mom has breast cancer," I told her.

"Damn," she said. "That's some hard shit. My dad had cancer. It nearly wrecked us."

Sanchez emerged from the hall, along with Cameraman George and the new sound guy, who wore Mossimo shirts. I phoned down to the control room. "Arthur, can you kill the lights? Jason and I are having an early night."

"Will do, Shanna." From his tone, I understood that he knew about Jason's mom.

That night we lay side by side, listening to cars pass on the street. The cast rarely had sex in the house, though once we caught Isaac showering with a girl from Tulane. Showers were off-limits for the crew. I whispered into his ear, "If you want to leave the house, I'll leave with you."

¤

Over the next few days, Jason was quiet and withdrawn. Up until this week, he'd been our community service coordinator: he'd emceed two fundraisers and was our HIV-awareness spokesperson. He was good at talking about disease prevention. Now, however, he spent a good deal of time alone, watching our fish tank and dangling his feet in the hot tub. On Tuesday at dusk we rode the St. Charles streetcar to Canal Street, accompanied by a cameraman, a sound guy, and a production assistant who asked bystanders to sign appearance waivers. The following night we sat by the Mississippi, watching the ferry transport cars from one bank to the other. "Look," I said, "I'm sure Sanchez would let you go for a couple weeks. He'd probably like the drama of it all. He's big on drama."

"It's like, I'm not even sure I should go. My mom would spend more time trying to convince me everything was OK than mentally preparing herself for surgery."

"You aren't going to be a distraction," I said. "Trust me on that."

"It's supposed to be fairly straightforward. Lumpectomy and light chemo."

"Geez," I said.

I laid my head against the firm padding of his shoulder and gazed at the moon-streaked water. The ferry sounded its horn twice before returning. We were very quiet sitting there, our coats buttoned to our chins. We were being filmed but pretended not to care. As kids, we'd suspected our lives might be TV shows. When the cameras finally showed up, we told ourselves it wouldn't take long to adjust.

As though on cue, Jason curved his arm around my shoulders just as the cameraman moved to film us from a different angle. The production assistant followed him, clipboard in hand. Jason let out a slightly exaggerated sigh, a signal the crew had yet to pick up. "You ever spent an entire night on a ferry?" he asked.

Along with the camera crew, we boarded the ferry, garnering the usual, inquisitive looks from strangers. When asked, the crew said, "A documentary." They never mentioned the show by name. We stood at the bow, our arms draped over the rail, and pretended to study the dark water. We did our best to look bored and complacent. After our second trip, the crew got off the boat, walked to the gray production van and drove away. Jason whispered: "A couple more runs for good measure and the night is ours."

We checked into the Ramada on Rampart. We undressed slowly. I removed his shirt, then undid the Velcro strap that held his wire and radio transmitter in place. I removed the *RW* pager from his belt and unbuckled his pants. We made love twice, car lights crawling across the curtains, the ice machine chattering in the hall. For a while we were regular people again. It would have been easier to fall in love in the regular world instead of *The Real World*, but we'd decided to make the best of it.

Around eight, we woke to the sound of my pager. As per cast requirements, I called the control room. Dave, the AM director, answered: "You two gave us the slip last night."

"From what I recall," I said, "it was one long ferry ride."

II

Though you'd never know this from the way the series was edited, I was a different person before I set foot in *The Real World*. I was a quiet, big-eyed college girl working through a biology program with no real plans beyond graduation. Up until my junior year, I'd never been in love and had only slept with three guys: one on prom night, one the summer after high school, and one my freshman year in college. Then I met David.

David was my lab instructor for microbiology. I don't know what drew me to him first. His voice, perhaps—his soft, deliberate voice addressing me from across our work station. Dressed in a lab coat, safety glasses flipped up on his forehead, he taught us how to perform gram stains. Using a copper loop he repeatedly demonstrated how to streak a plate until each of us could perform the procedure to his satisfaction. He had an odd way of smiling, as though he was particularly pleased with our progress.

I liked how he sat behind his teacher's desk, hands folded before him, eyes scanning the classroom while I talked to my group about a strain of bacteria we were trying to culture. Occasionally his gaze would fall on me, his face hopeful but firm, yet when our eyes met he turned away, pretending he'd been staring not at me but at the class in general. Even in those early weeks, I sensed he didn't love microbiology the same way our professor, Dr. Hines, loved it. David loved genetics and would often arrive with radiographs of human gene sequences, their images stenciled like elaborate bar codes across the flimsy negatives he let us look at after we finished our work.

I suppose I encouraged him, staying after class and making eyes. Occasionally I followed him to his office, which was decorated with gels he'd run earlier that year. At the time he was mapping out the genes of a famous stage actor. "We're looking for a sequence," he explained, "that he might share with other well-known actors from New York." Alone, he put his hand on my arm, just his fingertips really, feathering their way from my elbow to my wrist. It was such a soft, kind gesture I didn't know how to respond. I simply stood there looking at him. Turning to me he said, "I think we might get a tissue sample from De Niro next week."

"De Niro?" I asked.

"Yeah," he confirmed. "De *Niro*."

I fell in love slowly, lingering after class, letting him take me to his lab, where officially he was supposed to be studying genetic connections between frogs and lungfish—helping prove some theory his major professor was very much into. Away from school he was not the same person. He was nervous about his future, as was I, because he didn't know what he'd do after graduation. He was convinced he could find connections between chromosomes and careers. When I asked why fame, he said, "I suppose I could look for any predisposition—among accountants or something. But 'Scientist Finds Sequence for Accountants' doesn't sound as sexy as 'Scientist Finds Sequence for Fame.'"

I loved being with him, spinning down tissue samples and cycling them through the PCR machine. We worked under the assumption that we were destined to be here, predetermined by our genes to be biology students, to love pizza and diet Coke and even each other. We spent nights in the lab—I studied vertebrate physiology while he set up gel boxes—and in the morning we sat on the roof watching the sky lighten to violet, hoping to see satellites streaking through the far reaches of our atmosphere, their silver shapes leaving tiny vapor trails in their wake.

At the start of my senior year, I wanted to move in with him, perhaps plan a wedding, but David didn't feel the same. He avoided questions about our future, saying he just couldn't think about that right now. He was having trouble with his experiments. Using Harvard's genetic-personality markers as a guide, he hoped to find the links that had eluded him so far. By now, he'd acquired samples from Sharon Stone and Sylvester Stallone, Dustin Hoffman and Governor Jesse Ventura. At a conference in Utah, Robert Redford let him draw a small vial of blood. But even after Harvard issued an updated report, a partial mapping of the human genome, he failed to find the right connections.

Even after I graduated, he still kept long hours, stealing buffer solution from other professors, swiping extra boxes so he could run more gels. I thought I'd find a job as a lab tech but could only get work drawing blood at Veteran's Memorial. I worked from nine to five, arm after arm: strap, tap, poke. From magazines, I knew a man needed to feel successful. But after a while I felt ignored, abandoned to my life outside the academy. I resented him because he loved his lab more than he loved me. Even when I brought home my white phlebotomist's coat—a little costume so we could play doctor and nurse—he only spent a few hours with me before returning to the lab to dump fingernail clippings from some movie star into frozen culture.

I was at Mary's house when I filled out the application for *The Real World*. Both of us were a little tipsy on wine coolers. Though I'm not proud of it, I knew what I was doing. If David was more interested in fame than he was in me, *I'd* become famous. *I'd* become what he was searching for all along. But later that night as I drove home, I felt cords of regret tighten around my heart. I sat in my apartment, the lights off for at least twenty minutes, before I decided to take ham sandwiches to David's lab. For the first time in months I spent the entire night with him, the two of us making love on an old couch while a small current of electricity pulsed through his gel boxes, offering more results he was unable to use.

In the weeks that followed, I became moody, distracted. On those nights I was with David he was miles away—Darwin wandering through the lost island of Hollywood. At my lowest point, I bought a study book for the MCAT. I was lost and depressed. I put on a few pounds. But then *The Real World* called. The first round of interviews took place at the mall. I didn't tell David because I figured nothing would come of it.

On the morning of my second interview, I told him. We were sitting on the roof, the sky an asphalt haze above us. We were drinking merlot out of beakers we'd just run through the autoclave. I put my arm around him, already feeling the heaviness of what I needed to say. He listened patiently as I explained how I'd done these things behind his back, the application, the interview, the arrangements. A pale shadow of disappointment passed over his face. He lowered his eyelids then opened them.

"Are you saying you want to leave me?" he asked.

"I'm unhappy here. I don't like living like this. Separate apartments. You at the lab all night."

"You don't really understand what this means to me, do you?"

"I *do*," I insisted. "It means more to you than I do."

He looked at a car traveling up the distant freeway, its taillights fading into the darkness. "Why *The Real World?*"

"Because I wanted you to notice me," I said. "And I suppose I wanted to hurt you a little."

"I see," he answered. "Do you still feel like that?"

"Not really," I said. "But if they offer me the part, I want to go. I want to do something different for a while, see who I become. I don't like my life here anymore."

"I'll graduate in a year," he said.

"I know," I replied. "I know."

At the interview I wore a blue jacket and skirt, the same outfit I used to fetch my lousy phlebotomy job. Needless to say I was the only chick in a suit. The others had already envisioned their possible roles on *The Real World.* Without much trouble you could sort them into three camps: bad-girl sluts, good-time party queens, bisexual art chicks. I was in a camp of my own: college grad in troubled relationship.

I expected to be nervous, but the casting director, or CD as he was called, had a slow, smooth voice that calmed me. We sat in a small room along with his assistant, in front of a video camera set on a tripod. For a while he asked standard questions about my childhood, family, and college experiences, but about an hour into the interview, he began to pace, his face pinched in thought, as though my answers confused him.

"Be honest with me, Shanna," he said. "Most people want to do the show because it's easy fame. Four months in a cool pad with cameras on your tail. But from you, I'm just not catching that vibe. What makes you want to do this anyway?"

I looked at the camera, then looked away. I sat there, dressed in my best two-piece Jones number, realizing the success of the interview depended on my answer. "Because I want to spend some time away from my boyfriend. I want to see who I become on my own. I was kind of young when I hooked up with him."

At this the CD glanced at his assistant. He pressed his hands together prayerfully. "I believe we'll be getting back to you."

¤

We broke up slowly, David and I, dismantling our relationship as carefully as a failed chemistry experiment. Even after I moved to New Orleans, I still called him, slow, quiet conversations made from pay phones, but by now I was feeling better because I was rooming with Brandy. Before coming to the Big Easy, she'd broken up with her beau, too. "You know what he called me before I left?" she asked. We were sitting in the kitchen with Jason and the film crew. "He called me the New Orleans booty queen."

"What's a 'booty queen'?" I asked.

"Girl, you don't know what a booty queen is? It's a ho," she explained. "And do you see me getting hootchy-kootchy with any guys around here?"

"I don't see anyone getting hootchy-kootchy," Jason said.

"'Course not. With the cameras on you twenty-four-seven, who's going to be doing the down-and-dirty except some porn star? Last time I called, I told him I was seeing less action than Tootie saw on *The Facts of Life*."

"Last time I called David, that subject didn't come up."

"Shanna, you need to stop calling. It's like casting your mamma's pearls before swine."

"I know," I said. But every couple of days I walked down to the Circle K to use its pay phone. Brandy and I stood watch for each other, keeping an eye out for the gray production van because we didn't want these conversations taped.

Gradually I realized David was slipping deeper into the world of science, spending every night in the lab, a change of clothes under his workbench. With his time running out, he wasn't as picky about the samples he used. He was spinning down such has-beens as Clint Howard and Rosie Perez. Once he let it slip that he was working on Gil Gerard. "You know," he explained, "*Gil Gerard*—Buck Rogers from that old TV show."

"Oh," I said, then let our conversation drift into silence.

I suppose it was this, more than anything, that made me want to be a different person in New Orleans. *How* I wanted to be different, I wasn't sure. Prettier, funnier, more talkative? I could no longer see myself as the old Shanna, the one who pricked arms for a living and brought sandwiches to the lab. Brandy taught me how to do my makeup. I started to wear an anklet and even a little gold cross, just because I liked how it looked. At the end of my first month I asked David, "Do you ever miss me?"

"Of course," he said. But I heard a hesitation, a hum, the whirl of the centrifuge spinning vials behind him.

After I hung up, Brandy sauntered over, clucking her tongue in rebuke. "It's like I'm encouraging this behavior. I do lookout while you call the ex."

"On a suckiness scale of one to ten," I said, "a solid seven."

"My last phone call I give a five. I hung up before Thomas could push it any higher. You got to kick a dog *before* he bites you."

"That's my problem," I said. "I'm no good at hanging up."

"Girl, the line's already gone dead. You just aren't listening."

The following night Brandy and I were supposed to hand out condoms on Bourbon Street, but after we emptied our first bucket we returned to the house and got in the tub with Isaac and Jason. We drank Maker's Mark from a silver flask Isaac kept on him for show. I enjoyed drinking because it made me forget about my lousy life. My god, what a dork I'd been, hanging out in the *genetics* lab.

"The way I see it," Isaac said, "*The Real World* is always looking for troublemakers."

"And let me guess," Brandy said, "you're just the nigga to wear those pants."

"I'm not saying anything of the kind, dig? I'm just saying that you three ain't causing your share of trouble."

"Oh, I'm going to cause my share of trouble," I said. "You can count on that."

My friends stared at me in disbelief.

"I *am*," I insisted.

"Just wait until our reunion show," Jason said to Isaac. "See where you end up."

"Me?" Isaac said. "I was made for the big screen."

"Really?" Jason said.

Though I knew it was a bad idea, I started telling them about David's theory. I didn't say he was my ex, just that he was this guy I used to know back home who thought famous people had similar genetic sequences. "You know, like Gil Gerard and Robert De Niro," I said, but I wasn't explaining it right because no one seemed to understand. "It's this thing that's inside of you, you know, a bunch of genes. Like whether you get black hair or blond. And it just comes out. You can't help it. That's what he thought fame was."

"Girl," Isaac said, "I don't know what you're saying, but you sure are drunk."

"I'm not drunk," I said. "I'm just saying he had a pretty interesting idea."

Isaac rubbed his hands together enthusiastically. "Now what I suggest is a little game of T or D to get this train out of the station. No way to go wrong with that."

At this, Cameraman George moved to film us.

"Ain't no way I'm getting on that train," Brandy said. "You and Janice, sure, you can do the Truth or Dare thing, but you won't see any high-beam action from me tonight."

Isaac set the flask on the lip of the tub. "So tell me, with an attitude like that, how did you ever get through those cast interviews?"

"I said I was a level-headed girl and was going to be an accountant someday."

Isaac handed the flask to me. "I said I needed time away from my ex."

I turned to Jason. Only then did I notice he was looking at me. "Truth or Dare is your territory," he said to Isaac. He moved his foot against my leg, carefully raising it from my ankle to my calf. I moved my leg closer, hidden beneath the frothy surface of water, then I felt his hand touch mine.

Over the next few days I spent a good deal of time with Jason, sitting on our screened-in porch and sipping sweet tea. Like me, he didn't know what to do now that he'd graduated. He knew a lot about investments but hadn't been able to get a job at a broker's office, even as an assistant. He explained his situation in such a way that I felt he understood me—that he knew the best thing about my job at the hospital had been the white lab coat I got to wear every day. I never felt I had to impress him, which was a nice change from the way I'd felt with David.

That Thursday, while taping my weekly *RW* confessional, Sanchez asked me about him: "So tell me, Shanna, what's up with all that?"

"What do you mean?" I said. We were in the basement next to the control room, along with a cameraman and a sound guy.

"I mean, you've been spending a lot of time with Jason."

"We get along well."

"You're stonewalling me. You know how this works."

"Mum's the word," I said.

"You're breaking my heart. 'Mum's the word.' It's so protective. We're friends here."

I offered the camera a thin-lipped smile. "Mum," I whispered.

The cameraman began to laugh. Crew members were not supposed to react to the cast. "I think she's saying, 'mum,'" he said.

"Yeah," Sanchez said. "I got that part."

After that day, Jason and I had a film crew with us whenever we left the house. If millions of people were going to see me, I wanted them to see me like this, on the verge of love, wearing my little gold cross and anklet, walking around town with Jason at my side. We took Meals-on-Wheels routes together. We handed out literature on STDs in the French Quarter. We helped the local gay church schedule a Good Friday service called Out of the Closet and into the Tomb.

Like most boys I knew, Jason never really talked about love, but from time to time I'd catch him looking at me, his eyes so pensive I knew he had feelings for me. Twice he left flowers on my bed, and once, on a note card, he wrote: "If I get nothing else out of this whole experience at least I'll have met you." I hid the card in my purse, the one place I knew the crew wouldn't mess with it.

The following week I wrote David to tell him I was moving on. I listed reasons why our relationship hadn't worked: because I'd been intimidated by his accomplishments, because I'd felt young and naive around him, and then, in a moment of blinding honesty, I wrote because he could lower himself to sift through the genetic remains of Gil Gerard. I showed the letter to Brandy, who made me rewrite it. In the second version, I closed by admitting I'd always love him, then signed it "S." I thought a single initial might suggest a lingering intimacy.

"Girl, I'm proud of you," Brandy said, "for telling him off like that." We stood in the bathroom as Sandy, the production assistant, wired us with microphones and battery packs.

"We tore up that version of the letter," I said, "remember?"

"Still, you said you were finished. I'm the biggest hypocrite alive. I keep telling you to ditch your man, but I call mine every week."

"You do what your heart tells you to do," I said.

"Problem is, my heart's all fucked up. That's why I'm on the show. My heart's fucked up but I'm trying to make it good."

"Maybe we're all like that," I said.

"Raise your arms," Sandy instructed.

"Fuck," Brandy said, "I feel more like I'm on *Wild Kingdom* than on *Real World*. I'm the dopey little brown bear that Jim just downed. Now I'm being tagged and released."

III

For a while we fell into our own groove. Jason and I were dubbed the "responsible ones," though we snuck off every couple of days to have sex at a friend's apartment. Brandy was doing her best to stay with the twelve-step program. Isaac was hosting late-night disco parties for the Tulane students, most of whom showed up solely to get some screen time. Janice and Tully had taken to sunbathing in the nude out back, and Rich had taken his community service so seriously he turned religious on us. In short, Sanchez was eating it up. He even hired an extra crew to follow Rich as he went to church each Sunday, a Bible tucked under his arm, his hair perfectly parted.

As for me, I loved those weeks—those short, warm weeks nestled into March and April. I bought new clothes. I read some books. I lay around with Brandy, our faces slathered with cucumber masks. More than once, while Jason and I walked to our friend's apartment, we found a camera crew behind us, the sound guy using a special telescopic mike, but we didn't care. We were shy lovers. We did it under the covers. We turned off the lights even though the afternoon sun sliced through the blinds. After making love, we liked to sit outside, drinking Sam Adams and watch the moon levitate above the horizon.

The news about Jason's mom threw us all. Even Sanchez didn't know how to handle it. This was *The Real World* after all. We were supposed to be horny, drunk kids, falling in love, having fights. Cancer wasn't part of the program. Slowly we began to change as the regular world muscled back into our lives.

I don't mean that we changed in large ways, but in ways only the most regular viewers would notice. Janice, for example, started wearing her bathing suit again, as did Isaac. Tully had a regular girlfriend. Though she'd been the AA route before, Brandy began to carry one of their poker chips in her pocket. "This little white chip," she told me, "means Jack Daniels ain't my friend no more." Almost overnight I became aware of the cameras again. Then I realized a strange thing: I didn't want to be on TV anymore.

Each morning I found Cameraman George hovering over my bed. "Well, good morning," I said, but he wasn't allowed to answer. In the bathroom, I met up with Brandy, dressed in her leotard. Just that week, she'd started power walking. She held up her poker chip and kissed it. "Every day's a motherfucking gift," she said.

I rarely saw Jason before ten. He lingered at the breakfast table before taking a shower. Three days a week we had our Meals-on-Wheels route, and while cruising around the French Quarter I often took his hand, noticing that his fingers no longer curved around mine in that same special way. We didn't sneak off to our friend's apartment as often, and when we did I could tell he was troubled—not just about his mother but about other things as well.

One day, while eating po'boys by the river, I asked if he thought we'd be different people once we left *The Real World*. "I don't want to be," he said, then set his sandwich on a ripped paper bag we were using as a plate. He looked out at the water, his gaze on a boatload of tourists. "Thing is, Shanna, I was never very popular back home. I never organized anything. No one listened to me. I was sort of like everyone else."

"I was, too," I said. "I drew blood for a living." He sat there, his arms clasped around his knees. "I've been thinking maybe I've been caught up in this *Real World* thing a bit much. It was an easy escape from my old life."

I took his hand and held it. I couldn't remember any boy's hand I loved holding more than his. Together we watched an Irish wolfhound lope through the park. A pair of tourists videotaped each other. We checked the street for the production van, but saw only an unmarked cab. Slowly I faced him—dressed in his jeans jacket and white cotton T-shirt. His hair was combed back in a very businesslike manner, his eyes already focused on me. "What are you going to do about your mom?" I asked.

Absently, he ran his finger under my anklet. "I want to go see her."

I sat there quietly, afraid of what he might say.

"I'm going to leave." He checked my reaction. "Maybe next weekend."

"Oh," I said.

Without looking at me, he continued to play with my anklet, touching each of its three charms. "Did you mean what you said," he asked, "about coming with me?"

"I did," I said. "I still do."

"I could tell Sanchez I'll leave Sunday. You know, just me alone, like he expects." He leaned toward me. He took my hands again. "But we could slip out the night before."

¤

That night, after he talked to Sanchez, we went to my room and covered the lipstick camera on my bookshelf. We shut the door and blocked it with my desk. In bed, we began to kiss, lacy curves of moonlight slanting in around us. We made slow love, careful not to make noise, his eyes open as though he wanted to learn something about this girl he was taking home to meet his sick mother. I thought this meant something, making love in the house. There would be a record of it, a cameraman filming our closed bedroom door. Jason fell asleep early, his hands folded like an apple beneath his chin. As he lay there I sat at my window, looking at the neighborhood, rows of old Victorians out toward the river.

Around midnight Brandy returned, dressed in her favorite red dress, a black belt cinched around her waist. She looked at Jason, then me, her eyebrows arched with suspicion. "Did the crew finally give you some peace?"

"No one came inside. They know their limits."

"They don't know anything of the kind. How many shots of me do they need brushing my teeth each morning?"

We sat together, pillows pushed up behind our backs. I'd never had a sister, but imagined this was what it would be like. How I wanted to tell her about our secret departure. But the room was miked. Besides, I'd promised Jason I wouldn't.

¤

The following day, Sanchez made preparations for Jason's departure. He scheduled an extra crew to arrive Sunday morning and, in what I considered a fairly sleazy move, began asking the other cast members if they'd ever known anyone with breast cancer. Clearly, he was building "the breast cancer episode." During my weekly confessional, he knew enough not to ask me about it. Instead he asked how I'd feel once Jason was gone. I did my best to sound aloof: "Thing is, Jason and I both knew how things might work out. We're from different places. He has things to take care of. I can understand that."

"But Shanna," Sanchez said, "you two seem to have something special."

"That's what being on *The Real World* has taught me. You need to move on from one special experience to the next. Before I came here, I had something special with a boy back home, but I can't ever see myself dating him again either."

"You can't?"

"I think Jason and I are making that same move—slowly shifting toward friendship."

The following afternoon I helped Jason fold his clothes into his suitcase—his polo shirts, his jeans, the pair of Doc Martens we'd bought at the Riverwalk. When we were sure we were alone, we put my clothes into another suitcase then zipped it shut. "You sure you want me to go?" I asked. "What about your mother, the operation, all that?"

"I'm sure. We can stay with my sister until I figure something out."

That evening, as I walked Brandy to the AA meeting, I realized this would be our last trip together. By now I knew New Orleans as well as my hometown. I knew the alleys, the schools, the houses with little signs in their front windows: "*Real World* Go Home."

"You ever regret coming to New Orleans?" I asked.

"Girl, I never regret anything. I don't even regret falling in love with Thomas, dog that he is."

"You still going to be an accountant?"

"I think a regular job would be good for me. Pretty sure I could get into that nine-to-five shit." We stood at the entrance to the school where the AA meetings were held. The sky dimmed to the color of ash. Around us, the poker-chip brethren were making their way to the auditorium. "Why all the questions? You almost as bad as Sanchez. He goes on and on about what I think I'll make of myself."

I looked at her, her hair corn-rowed into braids, her hand holding her pocketbook. "There's something I need to know," I said. "You started drinking again?"

"Hell no."

"You been thinking about it?"

"You listen to Sanchez too much. He's always trying to stir the pot. He's one manipulative bastard."

"Have you?" I asked.

She put her hand around my arm, right at the muscle. "Girl, I'm always thinking about it. Course I am. But these lips know nothing but diet Coke."

"Good. I want you to be my accountant someday."

"Damn," she said. "You're worse than my momma."

That Saturday we had a going-away party for Jason, an impromptu event arranged by Isaac, of all people. He bought a cake and, with Janice, painted a sign that read: "Miss You, Big J." Beneath this they stapled a pink ribbon, the international symbol for breast cancer awareness. Aside from the cake and sign, this party differed little from other parties hosted by Isaac. Around 10:00 his friends showed up, many with cards wishing Jason well, though one boy punched Jason in the arm and said, "Age is but a number." Around 10:30 Isaac started up the disco, and by 11:00 Rich was talking to people about his belief in God.

A camera crew stayed with me as I ate cake and downed a beer. They were hoping to catch a big going-away scene, but I was doing my best to appear disinterested. On screen, I realized, I'd come off a little icy, but I didn't care because six hours from now I'd be driving west on I-10.

For the most part Jason was occupied talking to Isaac and Tully, though occasionally he glanced at me, his eyes cool and alert. I talked to Manning, then to Rich, who told me three people had accepted God since he'd begun his mission last month. When the music stopped, I put my arm around him. "You know," I said, "once Jason leaves, I hope you'll be supportive about Brandy's decision to attend AA. She'll need someone to take his place."

"I thought *you* were the one who was supportive," he said.

"Jason's been very supportive, too. I think Brandy needs all the support she can get. Your church believes in things like that, right?"

"Yeah, the church is very big on support."

I picked up my beer from the counter and drank from it. "Good," I said, "because I wouldn't want Brandy to be without it."

Toward the end of the evening, Jason danced with me. His eyes filled with a glassy sorrow as though this would be our last night together. He was a good actor. "Pretend I'm leaving tomorrow," he whispered. "Pretend this is our last night together."

As we danced, George the cameraman circled us for a closeup, but I didn't pay attention to him. My eyes were on Jason. I wanted him to remember this day, the very feel of it, slow-dancing beneath this mirror ball. I wanted him to remember what it was like to be here, in love, in this house. Who knew what the regular world would hold for us once we left?

At midnight, Isaac raised his glass to us. "To the brother who's leaving," he said. "Peace from the gods."

"Peace," Brandy said, then raised her diet Coke.

By now I'd noticed Jason was not quite himself. He was tipsy, but it wasn't just that. Nerves, I guessed. He kept picking up my hand, then placing it at my side. When the cameras turned on us, he let out an exaggerated sigh, which was my signal to be as boring as possible. We pretended not to notice Janice as she stripped down for the hot tub. We looked away while Isaac did the Funky Worm across the dance floor. When we were sure the cameras weren't on us, Jason draped his arm across my shoulders. "It's kind of weird to think all this will be pitched as a TV show."

"It is," I said.

"You know your old boyfriend, how he thought fame was something inside of you?"

"Yeah?"

"Fame is letting the world see the intimate parts of your life—then letting them think it's entertainment. That's what fame is. It's nothing more than that."

Just at that moment, Sanchez directed a cameraman to film us. We stood at the bar, drinks in our hands. We glanced at the camera and pretended to talk. I looped my arms around his back and acted like only now was I realizing how much I'd miss him. I could feel the make-believe truth of those emotions grow heavy inside my heart.

¤

At four in the morning I left a note under Brandy's pillow asking her to forgive me. We left through the backyard, under the bushes and over the fence, so our own security guards wouldn't see us. Once on the street, I sensed a change come over us, a certain ease I'd never really felt before. I was no longer in college. I was no longer a cast member. I didn't even have my stupid phlebotomy job anymore. We walked along narrow lanes lined with elms, past whitewashed Victorians and a junior high where we'd passed out health department brochures our first week here.

"Want to know what I keep thinking?" he asked. "I keep thinking about the expression on Sanchez's face when he finds out we've split."

"They'll find some way to edit it together. They always do."

"I don't think so," he said. "Not this time."

As we moved along First Street, I felt a closeness with him, pins and needles of the heart. I was no longer an adolescent. If I was making a mistake—and perhaps I was—at least I was making an *adult* mistake. He checked to see if I was still at his side, then took my hand. When we got to the car—a rented Ford Escort he'd hidden there that afternoon—I stopped him on the curb because he seemed nervous. I wanted him to know we'd be okay out here. We'd find good jobs, even if they weren't the jobs we most wanted. We'd live near his family. We'd have each other. I circled my arms around his back, bringing his body close. I kissed him full-on, my hands on his cheeks, our bodies moving against each other. "Where's that apartment when you really need it?" I asked.

"What's gotten into you?"

"It just feels great being out of that house—being in the regular world again." I cupped my hands behind his neck affectionately. "I really do love you. I've never felt quite like this about anyone."

"If I knew you'd be like this, I would've bailed weeks ago."

"It's strange. I guess I've felt like this all along. I was just scared to show it around the cameras. I didn't want them to own me that much."

"Show me now," he said and brought me into another kiss, bending me against the car, the top two buttons of his shirt open so I could see the slender curve of his chest. I ran my hand down the length of his stomach and over his jeans. "Just drive with me for ten minutes," he said. "First hotel we see, we're stopping."

Then I happened to look across the street. There, under an elm, I saw the gray production van parked at an angle, a good forty yards away, its tinted panel windows facing us. Sensing my anger, Jason followed my gaze. The van shifted from one side to the other, a small move, but telling. "Fucking Sanchez," he said.

We got into the car quietly and drove into the ashen darkness of our neighborhood. I felt the good feelings begin to leave us, but then Jason put his hand on my knee, saving the moment. The crew had the good sense not to follow us, but you can bet they were filming us drive away, a scene that would close the eighth episode, our Ford Escort moving up the street toward lives we could not imagine, as the music of Blink 182 faded into a commercial break.

The Yoshi Compound:
A Story of Post-Waco Texas

For weeks we'd been waiting for the ATF to arrive. Like most religious compounds in the Texas/Oklahoma area, we were hoping for a sizable show of force, two dozen federal agents done up in Kevlar/Spectra vests followed by media crews from all the networks, Fox in particular. But like every morning, as I drove to work I saw nothing but the cheery brown slope of the Texas foothills and Corporate Sano employees filling up the land with dried sewage shipped in from New York. I was doing my best to tune in my inner peace but was distracted by the knot of dread I felt pulsing like an irregular heartbeat somewhere in the general vicinity of my spleen.

I went through my special relaxation regime. I reminded myself that I was a child of most-high messengers, that the Dalai Yoshi himself had confirmed that I was at least two percent Cherubim. I popped the "Music of Bells and Finger Cymbals" into my tape deck, but the song didn't open my soul as Yoshi had suggested it might. Rather I was reminded of a club remix of "Puttin' on the Ritz" performed by a new-wave singer named Taco, a singer who'd fallen out of the music scene and was now working at a comic-book shop in London.

Again I tried to focus on the music, but when I rounded the final curve, my spirits sank as I saw the chain-link perimeter of the Yoshi Compound, its driveway empty except for the stacks of tires we'd heaped there street-riot style. There wasn't a federal vehicle in sight, not even one from the post office. I stopped at the gate and picked up a police-style body shield someone had left there, then continued down the thinly paved road that led to the outdoor exercise area.

The Yoshi Compound was a state-of-the-art facility complete with three cinderblock buildings, each outfitted with polycarbonate, shrapnel-resistant windows. We hoped for a significant standoff with federal agents, lasting a day or two, maybe even a week, but Yoshi's goals were mainly nonviolent. We wanted to save the world from that final, horrifying apocalypse, but in case we failed we had a fully outfitted pantry as well as three underground safe rooms. As with most local compounds, the riot gear was mainly a ploy for attention.

That morning Yoshi was seated on the public stage, wearing one of his saffron sarongs as his true followers gathered around him, some of the most faithful holding framed photos of his holiness above their heads. He was lecturing on the fourth scroll of heaven, a document that prophesied of a godless generation, a time of wickedness and self-destruction, and of the seven secret teachers who could save the world from its selfish ways. Even though he denied it, I thought Yoshi was one of these teachers, a man so holy he could straighten a crooked river if he so chose. "That which is most valuable," he said, "the world will ignore. The master comes before the teacher, and the teacher comes before the world."

All of his followers nodded. Clearly they understood the deeper meaning of his message, though I did not.

I walked toward the public stage, stepping around spent rifle casings, and stopped a good way from his audience, as I was not one of the
faithful but merely an employee of the Yoshi Compound USA. Whenever I was in Yoshi's presence I felt a warmth inside my chest, a peace
so mercurial I began to understand the basic flow of my life. I'd gone to
law school so I could work at the compound. I worked at the compound
so I could send my father a few dollars every week and so I could pay
back my student loans. But more importantly I worked here—or rather
I'd been *brought* here—so I could spend a few minutes each day learning from Yoshi. Because we were all descended from the Cherubim, he
liked to say, part of the pure Cherubic nature still rests within us. Only
then, at the peak of my self-understanding, did the bad feelings return,
cloud cover of the soul, as I remembered that I'd failed yet again. This
was the fifth day of Yoshi's "Heaven at Hand" lecture series, but still no
TV networks had arrived to bring his message to the world.

¤

We were all lawyers, all five of us having graduated from Northeast
Arroyo State Law School. Though I'd never quite understood why the
compound hired lawyers for these positions, our manager, Abe Fritz,
had once told me, "Never underestimate the value of a lawyer-client
confidentiality clause." I entered the Sacred Lamb Bunker, which was
also the office, still carrying around a sense of defeat that Yoshi often
remarked was nothing more than a sack of yak dung strapped to your
back. How I wanted one of my fellow workers to come over to me and
say, "It must be very difficult to hold the media relations/attorney position," but my coworkers sat at their desks, updating their resumes and
playing on the Internet. I leaned against the ballistic-grade steel door,
then took a few deep, soul-clearing breaths before I wandered over to
my cubicle.

My cubicle was next to Steve's. Steve was a short man in his late twenties who was fond of wearing concert T-shirts to work. He held the fund raising/attorney position, which meant he solicited charitable donations from Yoshi followers worldwide in addition to managing our Internet casino, Vegas Gold Online. I often felt sorry for Steve because he'd once worked for the DA's office, but after the DA's nephew graduated from law school, they got rid of Steve by claiming his urine test came back borderline positive. He sat hunched over his computer, working on that morning's *Vegas Gold Newsletter*, which went out to over twenty-thousand Internet gamblers via e-mail. The moment I sat down, he leaned over—I thought he might ask the correct spelling of a particular word, as he was a terrible speller—but instead he elbowed me in the ribs. "Fritz says your ass is grass if you can't get a Fed here by sundown."

"Ha ha," I said. I hoped he was joking.

Tami, who held the book editor/attorney position, simply rolled her eyes. I rolled mine back, believing she might be flirting, but she returned to her resume, changing the font, then printing copies onto the hand-laid paper we saved for Yoshi's personal correspondence with high-level donors.

I searched the AP site, as I did each morning, for regional stories submitted by other compounds. Pretty much every compound had a PR guy like me who typed up press releases and submitted news items reported from a quote/unquote objective standpoint. I found three or four stories, all of which dealt with the usual themes, namely the accumulation of guns and riot gear. The Branch Delphians went so far as to add the heading, "Compound Declares Itself Independent Nation, Seeks Nuclear Capability," but everyone knew the Delphians were a bunch of wackos who believed the second coming would be achieved via spaceship.

Still, there was something about their article that gave me the impression no news stories would be picked up today, particularly if they were about the "usual topics." What a shame, because I'd already composed half my article in my head, a personal-interest piece about Texas natives stopping by our compound to witness the followers of Yoshi practice at our FBI-style shooting range. I'd been working on this for a day or two, noting how cars—when there were cars—occasionally slowed as they passed the front gates to get a good look. Often the people yelled things like, "You're all a bunch of frigging retards," but I planned not to include that. Rather, I'd have people stopping at the roadside to talk with individual followers through the chain-link fence, while Daniel Rami, the range foreman, did a safety inspection of each rifle. In my version, I'd have these onlookers ask questions such as, "What's the worldwide importance of the Cherubim's message?" and, "How will we know the seven secret teachers?" while the followers of Yoshi slipped preprinted tracts through the fence into their waiting fingers. But already I understood that I'd have to trashcan this idea, much the same way I'd had to trashcan certain defenses in law school hours before the practice trial.

I had a couple of ideas to fall back on—"Yoshi Compound Takes Position on Drinking Water Standards" and "Virgin Mary Appears in Clouds above Gun Range"—but neither of these ideas had the force to attract the attention of the Feds. For at least twenty minutes I walked around the office, drinking cup after cup of coffee, even though Yoshi warned against the abuse of caffeine and other diuretics. I looked out the thick front window. From my vantage point I could see Daniel Rami setting new paper targets against bales of hay; I could see little children gathered around Mrs. Taylor, the elementary school teacher; I could even see Yoshi's private altar through a reinforced window opening into the Sacred Heart Bunker. I imagined Yoshi there, kneeling on his camel's hair pillow, asking God to open his mind so he might better understand the fourth scroll of heaven.

Standing there, I asked something of God as well. I asked that he would give me an idea the papers would run, something that would cast the Dalai Yoshi in a warm, personal light and cause at least one Fed to visit our fine compound before sundown. But after five minutes, I felt no closer to an article than I'd been an hour before. I also realized that I was staring in the general direction of Tami, noticing something about the way she addressed each manila envelope before slipping in a resume. Apparently she sensed this, too, a momentary connection, because she looked my way. "God Boy," she said, "quit stalking me."

I returned to my cubicle defeated and watched Steve ratchet down our casino's odds one more time, using the site's SafetyBet software. Right then, just as I thought I might quit, I envisioned the first piece of my article, as plain as the crimson dot between Yoshi's eyes, a paragraph or two that I might expand into something worthy of publication.

In the article I started out by pretending I was a freelance reporter who'd come to Texas for the express purpose of uncovering the financial life of the compound. I looked for just the right words to express my surprise at finding such elaborate and well-constructed apocalypse-ready bunkers. I marveled at the military-issue Humvee that was used whenever Yoshi went to town. I looked for someone to talk to about the financial management of the compound. I considered "interviewing" Steve, but on more than one occasion he'd told me, "If you want to quote someone, quote yourself." So I, the reporter, pretended to interview me—the *real* me, that is, Tony Foley, compound employee.

As Tony Foley, I explained how the compound was started with seed money provided by the Yoshi Group International. From that we purchased the land as well as the first two bunkers. Since the compound has been operational, it has become mostly self-supporting, relying on direct contributions as well as profits from book sales and our Internet casino. I listed a number of our best-selling titles, such as *On Stress* and *The Dalai Yoshi Discusses the Afterlife*. Our Internet casino, I remarked, was a joint venture with the Costa Rican brotherhood. Although some consider gambling an "immoral" activity, the proceeds from the venture furthered the Dalai Yoshi's teachings and various peace conferences held throughout the world.

Sitting in my cubicle, I started to feel very good about my article. Not only that, I had a renewed sense of confidence in myself, a good spiritual glow. I believed other employees noticed this because they treated me with a certain deference missing from most of our daily interactions. Tami actually *asked* for my tape dispenser before grabbing it off my desk. Steve offered to credit my casino account with ten bonus dollars before he went off to take some prescription headache medicine in the break room/harmony chapel. When he returned, he decided to order pizza and even asked what toppings I wanted on my portion.

"I'm going to work through lunch," I said.

He stood there in his Marilyn Manson T-shirt and jeans looking somewhat put out. "Tami and I are going to *buy* the pizza," he explained. "You can eat it at your desk."

"Okay, pepperoni," I said, "or whatever."

As he walked away, I had a small realization about life, something Yoshi would call a "purposeful soul bubble." These people respected me because I respected myself, and I respected myself because I was able to write a good article, one that could run in either the Lifestyles or Business section of any paper. I spent the rest of the morning finding the right words to present the Yoshi Compound as a place of spiritual discovery as well as a financially savvy nonprofit organization. I worked through my morning break and even through the sitar/meditation break because I felt a peace inside me, a peace that couldn't be shattered no matter how many dirty looks Tami threw my way, no matter how many quote/unquote official e-mails Steve sent about my casino account supposedly being overdrawn.

¤

I suppose Steve and Tami would've treated me better if they'd known more about my life—for example, if they'd known my mother had meticulously cut each of my father's war medals in half before divorcing him or that she'd stuck his pet bird, Lulu, in the oven for a few minutes before he was able to rescue her. As a child, I couldn't understand why my father didn't retaliate by bashing in her car window or locking her out of the house instead of sitting on our back porch and looking out at the tall, flat-topped mountains while Lulu, a yellow-naped Amazon, cleaned the small hairs on his neck. I often thought Lulu was the reason my father was able to pull through the divorce so well, Lulu whose tail feathers never grew back. But one evening, months after the divorce, he told me that all people have important choices to make in this life. "Son, you can concentrate on good feelings or obsess about the bad. That's what they don't teach you in school—you choose the person you become."

I left my father that night with a big sadness in my chest, a sadness much larger than the one I felt after I'd watched *Brian's Song* on TV. In the bathroom I took a good look at myself, my ripped T-shirt and my hair that I was trying to grow out like Dee Snider's, the lead singer of Twisted Sister. Even though my father didn't specifically point this out, I knew I'd been obsessing about bad feelings. Over the next few weeks I cut my hair and started wearing shirts with collars. I woke early and read inspirational sections from my father's copy of *The One-Minute Manager*. Eventually I sold my heavy metal albums and purchased music by popular new-wave artists, such as Wham! and the Jets, whose lyrics didn't make me think about how angry I'd been the year before.

Years later, in law school, I wanted to become a trial lawyer assigned to juvenile offenders so I could help them both with their legal difficulties and with managing their feelings, but I wasn't very good at case law. My greatest strengths turned out to be with legal briefs. I could proofread like no one's businesses. Even my professors gave me their briefs so that I might tighten up a phrase here and there. But after graduation, these same professors were unwilling to take me on in their law firms, so I went out on my own, checking the want ads in *Law Jobs Weekly* until I found the position at the Yoshi Compound.

Initially I was hired to help sway community opinion about a school vouchers program. Abe Fritz believed the compound might save tens of thousands each year exchanging vouchers for tax dollars. For a while I thought we'd be able to pass such a measure, our county being so small, but we lost on a technicality. The county threw out a couple hundred ballots cast by Yoshi's followers because for one reason or another they were not eligible to vote in the state of Texas.

By this time I was making friends at the compound, especially when I brought in my copies of *Law Jobs Weekly* as I no longer needed them. Steve asked me for only half my profits in exchange for teaching me how to sign up for bonuses at other online casinos, and after lunch Tami would tell me about having sex with our accountant/attorney, Randy Morgan, inside the Light of the World Bunker—that is, until Abe Fritz fired Randy for outsourcing the accounting work to a college student who knew how to use Quicken.

We were somewhat close, me and my fellow workers. Each Friday we had a potluck. Steve would bring in a bag of chips, Tami the soda, Arnold (Randy's replacement) the napkins. I had the most difficult job, the main course and a vegetable side dish, but I didn't mind the work because I knew how much my coworkers enjoyed my cooking. Each Thursday night I spent hours putting together something a little extra special, relying on those recipes I'd picked up from my dad, such as chicken cacciatore and salmon en croute. We ate on the back patio from which we could see methane rainbows shimmering above the Corporate Sano foothills. My friends would make little jokes about Yoshi's followers and even about Yoshi himself, but after lunch they'd all compliment me, saying things like, "We should do this twice a week" and "I'm glad you weren't axed over that ballot thing."

Within a few months I understood the basic layout of our office. From time to time, Steve would ask me to help with the *Vegas Gold Newsletter* and once even asked me to write to Gamblers Anonymous to see if we could purchase a mailing list under the auspices of the Yoshi Compound USA. Tami moved on to Arturo, the book-order fulfillment specialist who had been a licensed attorney in El Salvador, before she moved on to Sam, the Web designer/attorney. Often they would sneak into the supply room during break only to emerge an hour or so later, their clothes wrinkled, little welts on Tami's neck and arms. I couldn't help but think Tami would be happier with a person like me, one who took his job seriously and knew how to respect a woman. Often I would walk by her cubicle, an extra cup of coffee in my hand, and comment on the fine work she'd been doing with Yoshi's books. Her editorial suggestions had made Yoshi's message considerably easier to understand.

"You actually *read* his books?" she asked.

"I read the pages you edited."

She appeared pleased, though confused, and smiled good-naturedly before highlighting another position advertised in the *Law Jobs Weekly* I'd brought her that morning.

After that day, Tami would occasionally drop off a chapter or two on my desk. "Perhaps with your help, Yoshi's message can be even clearer," she'd say before talking with Sam about innovative marketing ideas she'd had in the shower that morning. I always read the chapters with great care, checking each paragraph to make sure it contained no run-on sentences or extra words. Yoshi loved to throw in extra words here and there, but once they were trimmed away, you could see the simple beauty of his message. Yoshi believed that the Cherubim had visited earth some forty thousand years ago and through advanced biological engineering techniques had mixed their genetics with those of early man, producing Cherub/Man hybrids. These hybrids became the founders of many ancient civilizations, such as Egypt and Mesopotamia, thereby spreading the genetic material of the Cherubim through the human gene pool. For hundreds of years, the world worked toward peace, finding joy in works of visual art and music, but over time, people lost their Cherubic nature. In fact, Yoshi believed some people had less than one-half of one percent Cherubic blood nowadays, which was why people found it so difficult to follow their better nature.

When I came to this passage, I put the manuscript down. I was seated at my cubicle, my news story, "NRA Gives Yoshi Service Medal," only half-finished, yet I could write no more that day. I was confronted with something I felt was truth—truth in that larger sense—about who I really was and what I was meant to do with my time on earth. I believed my father had been trying to tell me something similar that night on the porch, but within Yoshi's cleaned-up paragraphs I understood the message of my basic humanity so clearly that I was moved to stand at the window, hands clasped behind my back. I looked out at our compound, particularly at Daniel Rami, who taught new converts how to suit up in body armor. For months I'd considered this a fine job for a new lawyer, a job that would not only give me experience as an attorney but also as a publicist and office assistant, but now I saw the large hand of fate working in my life. I'd been guided to the Yoshi Compound so that I might understand this about myself, so I might hold this one crystal of knowledge. My good nature was a very small part of my overall body, only two percent, and therefore I'd have a difficult time following its impulse. The Cherubic message was a message against war and chaos, a message that said the human race held destiny in its hands. Yoshi was trying to save people from themselves.

When Tami returned from her meeting, she asked me to rub her feet because she hated wearing high heels. I rubbed them, believing that in some small way I was beginning to let the Cherubic message have an effect on me. I was performing a service for another person, even though this other person had legs and feet so perfectly formed I knew she must have at least three percent Cherubic blood in her body. When Abe Fritz returned from his meeting with Yoshi, he looked at us. "Tami," he said, "stop teasing the animals." Then he walked off to his office.

That very week I began to include little notes to my father about the Cherubic message. I told him that goodness resides in a very small portion of our bodies, in some cases only one-half of one percent, and that it is hard to follow the prompting of our Cherubic blood. Often I remarked how grateful I was that he'd set me on the right path so early in life, during those tender teenage years, and that he'd helped guide me to a moral and upright profession, such as law, that dealt with ethics and justice. Each week I included whatever money I could afford, though often it was only forty or fifty dollars, and each week he wrote back a note of gratitude, though once he said something I found confusing. "Tony," he wrote, "sometimes I feel I did you a disservice. Perhaps I should've taken your mother for all she was worth, especially after she put my bird in the oven."

At first Tami was very enthusiastic about my conversion experience, always asking my opinion about the manuscript chapters Yoshi asked her to edit. We would sit in the break room/harmony chapel while Sam eyed us somewhat jealously from the water cooler. As I explained the basic message of each chapter, I felt that she was beginning to see me for who I was, a simple man who did his best to make it in the world. "So let me get this straight," she asked, "the Cherubim kind of had sex with these pre-Egyptians then gave them the blueprints for the pyramids?"

"That's why the Egyptians were the first truly advanced civilization."

"But sex?"

"Not quite sex. A genetic mixing that human technology is not yet able to understand. Then the Cherubim gave the Egyptians a moral code to develop their better nature."

She regarded me with eyes so deep in thought I believed she was reconsidering her place in the universe; then she placed her hand on my shoulder to steady herself. "What the fuck was I doing in law school?" she said. "I should have stayed a bartender." With that, she walked off, shooting a look of consternation at Sam, a look that meant he should meet her in the supply room. For the next twenty minutes, they stayed in there, running the Xerox for cover-up noise. But I knew a woman like Tami would never find what she wanted in the supply room. She needed a man with a larger spirit, a man who was able to see the good things this world had to offer. Like so many people of our generation, she'd been blinded by Hollywood feature films and network TV that told us cheap sex was the answer to so many of our deeper problems.

That night I went home with a heavy heart. How I wished I lived at the compound in one of the nicely decorated bunkers, that I could stay up late while one of the more advanced followers explained to me how this planet had worked itself into such a predicament. It seemed so simple, the basic Cherubic message, that we all needed to take better care of our neighbors, that we should value other people as much as we valued ourselves, but with our Cherubic blood diluted as it was, people found that message difficult to understand, let alone follow. I fell asleep early that night, looking at a photo on my wall of my father and Lulu, both of them wearing red sombreros he'd bought on a cruise.

In a dream, I saw my younger self, that teenaged boy with long, stringy hair, but then as I followed him around my old house, I watched the scenery change to a desert lit by a dim moon. I'd never seen a desert as vast and as rocky as this—no roads, no outlet malls, no high-tension wires draped between poles. I felt very alone, somewhat cold, but then I noticed a man walking toward me. At first I believed he was Yoshi because he was so old, his hair white, but as he drew close I realized he was someone else, mainly because of his dark face, his white beard, and the absence of a crimson dot between his eyes. He regarded me with confusion, two stone slabs tucked under his arm. I regarded him as well, the two of us like animals caught in the moonlight.

The following morning I drove to work a little faster than usual, pushing my Escort slightly over the speed limit, because I believed my dream might be an omen, a sign to let me know the Feds would soon arrive at our compound, followed by the media who would bring Yoshi's message to the world. But when I arrived the only strange car I found was a large Cadillac used by representatives of the Costa Rican brotherhood whenever they visited on business. I stood near the outdoor exercise area listening to Yoshi for a few extra minutes—he spoke on the worldwide family of man—but not even that could cheer me up. I walked into the office just as two large men dressed in dark suits and sunglasses exited and continued to the Cadillac. One of them, the driver, took a cigar from his coat pocket and set it in the corner of his mouth.

That morning when I visited Tami at her cubicle, she was buying cosmetics online and pretending I wasn't standing next to her. When I asked if Yoshi had any new chapters to revise, she told me she'd already given them to Sam, but maybe I could have them later, then dismissed me by shrugging her shoulders. Already I understood the problem. She'd been confronted with the truth of her existence, that human beings were divided in nature, being both Cherub and flesh, and that they had a responsibility to follow their Cherubic leanings so that they might forgive each other and make an effort to better respect everyone they met on a regular basis. Human beings must also look for ways to improve the world and not damage each other, but for Tami to do these things, she'd need to stop meeting Sam in the supply closet and no longer smoke special cigarettes out back with Steve, especially when the compound children were present. No longer would she be able to ridicule all the things Yoshi had to say. Rather, she'd need to look inside herself and cultivate the good feelings hidden there. I returned to my cubicle crestfallen, only to have Steve say, "Bad news, Tony. The computer tells me your casino account is overdrawn again."

That day I wrote a special news article in which the compound was quote/unquote visited by a marksman specializing in the use of armor-piercing bullets. I did an extra good job on each sentence, finding just the right words to describe our FBI-style shooting range, because I wanted the article to be published. If it was published, the Feds might read it. If the Feds read it, they might storm our compound along with the media, then the world would have a chance to hear Yoshi's message, carefully culled into fifteen-second sound bites Abe Fritz had already circulated to news organizations. And if more people accepted Yoshi's message, then people like Tami wouldn't feel so awkward accepting their Cherubic nature. But no papers picked up my armor-piercing bullets story. Neither did they pick up my next one, "Compound Hacks into Government Website," which featured a black-and-white photo of me staring intently at my computer monitor.

Though I'd had some early success with articles on land mines and guns purchased from the Kurds, I was losing my touch. Moreover, my coworkers' sentiments began to turn against me. No longer did they ask me to cook the main course each Friday. Instead, they suggested I pick up two buckets from KFC or buy a frozen lasagna. And since I was bringing frozen entrees, Steve said I should pick up the chips as well.

In truth, I was surprised how dismissive my coworkers were, considering me as crazy as any of the Branch Delphians, when all I wanted was to improve myself and look for the good in other people. Using ideas from *Yoshi and Our World*, I tried to explain to my fellow attorneys that I wanted to be a better person, to be more understanding, to cultivate peace in small ways, but even Arturo, our El Salvadorian refugee, shook his head in consternation. "Law school in this country," he said, "must be very different than law school back home. No wonder I cannot be a lawyer here."

By then I was eating most of my lunches alone, except for Fridays when I brought in the main course and chips. I would linger by the outdoor stage and watch Daniel Rami instruct new converts on passive resistance techniques used at other compounds. Often I looked for Yoshi. Except for one brief conversation, during which he smiled at me, I rarely saw him. One lunch hour when I was feeling particularly low, Garret Parks, a long-time follower, sat next to me. He was dressed in his new advanced-seeker sarong, his face set in an expression of otherworldly peace. When I asked why people had such difficulty accepting Yoshi's message, he turned to me, his eyebrows lowered in irritation. Only then did I remember he'd taken a week-long vow of silence.

That night I drove home slowly, stopping only once to mail a letter to my father. I heated up a can of soup and reread sections in *The Dalai Yoshi Discusses the Afterlife* that I hadn't understood the first time. I wondered at how departed souls passed through purifying water and at God's infinite justice assembled into a dominos game. I tried to imagine God with his ivory dominos, but before long I fell asleep, stretched out on my couch. I was lowered again into a landscape of darkness, the air turning cold before I realized I was in the desert again, only now the ground was covered with a thick, weedy grass. Distant trees opened to a star-speckled sky, and moonlight bled across the horizon like the aura of an adult Cherub. I wandered for a good ten or twenty minutes, picking up little rocks and tasting them, before I saw the old man, two tablets pinned under his arm. He looked at me across the desert grass. A weakness opened in my chest, a sense that I might never fully regain my Cherubic nature. Then the old man did something unusual; he made a shushing sound, and everything—birds, frogs, even the wind—was quiet.

Over the next few weeks I made significant steps toward improving myself. I no longer rolled through stop signs. I was careful not to speed and not to change lanes without first signaling. When I went to the supply room I got supplies for everyone. In my own way I was letting the Cherubic message take hold of me. Soon my friends began to anticipate my good deeds. "Next time you're making supply closet rounds," Tami said, "get me some large paper clips." I began to picture a world in which we served each other. I pictured a world where the goodness of Yoshi's message ran through everyone's heart. Wars could be avoided, suffering minimized, an overwhelming sense of futility pushed aside. But already I knew such a world could not be achieved on this earth, at least not while people had so little Cherubic blood.

By the time Yoshi began his "Heaven at Hand" lecture series, I'd noticed small changes in my friends, little gestures that indicated they, too, might be responding to their Cherubic nature. From time to time, Steve offered me one of his special headache pills, and though I never accepted, I appreciated his offer. Once Tami brought me a box of staples from the supply closet. When I thanked her, she said, "Those don't fit my stapler." But more importantly, I saw how she looked at me, a sadness in her eyes, as though she were thinking, I'd be better off with a man like Tony. Still she teased me, calling me "God Boy" and "Dickhead," but I believed that these insults pained her now, that they helped her understand how far she'd wandered from a true Cherubic lifestyle, because as Yoshi said, "Human beings can only understand their broken natures by acknowledging the bad deeds they do to each other."

During this same period, my news stories suffered. No longer was I able to attract the careful attention of local papers. I tried with such stories as "Yoshi Patents Plastic Explosive" and "Compound Hires Government Chemist," but nothing worked, not even my offer for a real reporter to tour the compound. Each time Abe Fritz walked past my desk, I was reminded of my failure: without effective PR, the Feds would never notice us, and without the Feds, how would Yoshi's message ever reach the world? More than once I browsed online bookstores, looking for a work that would discuss the PR tactics of Gandhi or Martin Luther King, but never was I able to find such a thing. I continued as best I could, writing one or two articles a day, listening to Yoshi's lectures whenever I could, helping Steve register new online casino accounts in my name so that he could earn referral bonuses.

¤

On the day I wrote "The Financial Life of the Yoshi Compound," I felt a respect for my work I hadn't felt in months, not since I'd been appointed head proofreader for the *Northeast Arroyo State Law Review*. I remembered the first lesson that any good compound PR man learns: think outside the box. That was just my problem; I'd been too involved in compound business to see my work from a fresh perspective. I'd been doing what every compound PR guy had been doing, attacking the problem head-on. But with "Financial Life," I was able to mention a good deal about our arsenal without making that the subject. I'd found a "side door for a good cause" as Yoshi liked to say. When I told Abe Fritz the title, he only shook his head, then returned to his desk.

I walked around the office believing that I was making a significant contribution, one that might help foster peace in the world. I felt satisfaction settle inside me, a warm light that began to break up my internal clouds. Right now, I imagined, many newspaper editors were reading my article on the AP Internet site.

Steve and Tami seemed to notice a change in me because more than once I found them following me with their eyes, a certain expectation etched into their faces. When I returned from the supply closet bearing two extra rolls of Scotch tape, Steve asked, "Aren't you ever going to eat the pizza we got you?" And there, on top of my inbox, was a paper plate holding two slices. I was touched. I sensed an electricity between us, a suspicion that my coworkers were finally yielding to their Cherubic blood.

I took my lunch to the picnic tables we saved for compound guests, such as irate parents. I ate slowly while, across the compound, Daniel Rami instructed new recruits how to properly adjust a gas mask. We hoped never to need the masks but knew how good they'd look in photos. I'd eaten one slice when I felt a turning in my stomach, a chemical heat. Only then did I wonder how long the pizza had been sitting in my inbox.

I pushed the other slice aside and thought I might just sit here, soaking up some of this good Texas sun, when I noticed Steve and Tami beside me, sharing a cigarette. Steve looked a little taller, as though his body had been stretched, and for some reason he was upset that I hadn't finished my pizza. "I'm just not that hungry," I said.

"You feeling okay?"

"Ready to start another article," I assured him.

He turned to Tami, then back to me. "Still not hungry?"

I shrugged, but Tami understood. "See," she told him, "you did it wrong."

I smiled as they left because I was lightheaded. I stayed in the sun, hoping this feeling would pass, and considered ideas for my next article. It was strange, this sensation, much like listening to my favorite new-wave band, Scritti Politti, and trying to understand their heavily accented lyrics. For a good ten minutes I imagined a new article in which Texas natives watched the followers of Yoshi practice at the gun range, but then remembered I'd trashcanned this idea hours ago.

When no other ideas came, I made my way to the visitors' chapel. I said hello to everyone I passed, even those people I didn't know, so strong was my Cherubic nature that afternoon. Once inside I was drawn to the votive candles. I picked up two and examined them, their little balloons of flame held down by a wick. How good their heat felt. By accident I spilled wax onto my arm. Strangely that felt good, a pleasant burning, and so I tipped a little more, until I had an unusual squiggle scalding my arm.

I fell asleep little by little, stretched out on prayer pillows, my body growing heavy. At first I didn't know what was happening, but then I understood that my Cherubic blood was expanding, just as Yoshi said it would, and that its expansion would cause me to change somehow. Before I knew it, I was in my dream desert eating rocks, only now I knew the rocks weren't rocks but bits of hard bread. The old man was beside me, picking dirt from his bread before eating it, so I did the same. When we ran out of bread, he sat beside me, his eyes so pretty and brown. Then he did something I didn't expect: he handed me his tablets, indicating that I should carry them a while as we walked off in search of food.

When I woke up, I thought Abe Fritz was beside me, ready to fire my ass, but gradually I came to realize it was Yoshi holding my hand, smoothing the hairs on my burned arm. His touch was very gentle, much like my father's, and seeing him there, I understood that my earlier premonition had been correct. My Cherubic blood had thickened, for as Abe Fritz once told me, Yoshi doesn't bother with the two-percenters.

Only when Yoshi stepped aside did I see the other people with him, some of his most advanced students, among them Daniel Rami and Garret Parks. They were arranged in a semicircle, eight of them in all, their hands clasped respectfully across their stomachs. Yoshi gestured at my burn mark, which caused his students to lean forward. "Burn," I tried to say, but the word didn't come out right.

"Yes, yes," replied Yoshi, then rolled back his own sleeve, revealing white skin except for a scar that was the twin to the mark on my arm.

"Only two percent," I told him.

He placed a steady hand over my heart. "Not two," he said, "five. Maybe six."

I tried to explain that it was only wax, a fresh burn, but Yoshi wouldn't listen. He helped me to my feet and placed me with his students, two of whom put their arms around me because I was having trouble standing under my own power. "God marks us in strange ways," Yoshi said.

For the next fifteen minutes, I felt as though I were walking through water, my legs stiff and unyielding. I wondered if this was how it had been for the other advanced followers, this strangeness with the body after their Cherubic blood had thickened. Gradually I got used to standing on my own and stopped blinking so much. Had I been given a new mind, one that would only consider my higher duties? I considered this for a while, but then my old worries returned. I remembered I should be writing a second AP article. When I saw that the sun was low in the sky, I realized Abe Fritz would be pissed, not only because I'd fallen asleep but because I was fraternizing with the advanced followers.

Still, I was compelled to be with them, these eight men in their purple advanced-seeker sarongs. Though I was still in my white shirt and khakis, I believed I was becoming one of them, that these men had the ability to understand the world as I understood it. We wanted to bring peace to our troubled planet. We didn't care if people ridiculed us. How could they understand us without guidance?

We sat for a while at the picnic tables reserved for visitors while Yoshi talked about the importance of postmillennial thought and postmillennial action. Though I had trouble following his logic—he mentioned Kierkegaard a lot—I figured he was talking about the Golden Rule more or less, so I nodded along with the advanced followers and tried to remember a few key phrases I could look up later. Yoshi was discussing the unfinished fifth scroll of heaven, which involved the "anger of nations," when I first saw my coworkers assembled outside the Sacred Lamb Bunker beside a sign that read "Check Ammo at the Door."

I looked at their confused faces. I waved, but no one waved back, not even Tami, whose eyes held a visible trace of regret. Surely she understood I wasn't like the other attorneys in our office. I was trying to find the goodness in life.

When Abe Fritz approached, taking firm, decisive steps across the dirt, Yoshi rose to meet him. They talked in the shade of the compound water tower, and though I couldn't hear most of their conversation, I knew Abe was explaining what a failure I'd been—an attorney who hadn't placed a story in over a month, not even with the *Frontiersman,* a pro-NRA publication out of San Antonio. I heard little bits of their argument, such as Abe Fritz saying, "I don't care if he's *one-hundred*-and-six percent Cherubim." Each word made me feel smaller, undeserving of Yoshi's attention. I'd had an important job, and I'd failed at it. I was sorry I didn't bring the Feds to our compound. I would've given anything for Yoshi's message to have the national attention it deserved.

I closed my eyes, hoping to find my inner peace, but when I opened them, the world had gone quiet. Abe and Yoshi were no longer arguing. My coworkers had stopped gossiping. They were all staring at me, their faces wide and curious—that is, I believed they were staring at me until I turned around and saw what they were really looking at. At the front gate, two men dressed in blue suits stood by a Ford Taurus, clearly an unmarked government vehicle. The taller man raised binoculars to his eyes while the other snapped photos using a digital camera outfitted with a long-barrel lens. They stood there for quite a while, taking notes and talking. The taller man went so far as to pace off the distance between our gate posts before leaving.

I watched their car move up the road, past the power plant, past the old reservoir, and stop at the base of the Corporate Sano foothills.

Only then did I see the other cars assembled, what looked like four or five similar Tauruses, all of them parked at the side of the road.

¤

Rather quickly the entire compound shifted into a Code One alert signaled by a low, intermittent chirp broadcast over the PA system. The nonessential staff, such as Steve and Tami, left, as did compound guests. Daniel Rami placed three nonfunctioning fifty-gauge rifles near the gun range, each outfitted with a laser scope and silencer, while a few new converts went about the perimeter arranging police-style body shields near the fence. Some senior members draped homemade signs across the Light of the World Bunker, bedsheets holding such messages as "The Truth of the Cherubim Is Inside You" and "The Earth Is in Our Hands." Yoshi retired to his private altar, as did many of his advanced followers. As for me, I could have left along with my coworkers, but chose to stay.

I found that the office door had not been secured, though Arturo should have locked it before leaving. At my desk, I noticed that my computer screen was filled with new e-mail messages. Many were to alert me that my Vegas Gold account was overdrawn, but a few concerned my "Financial Life" article. One subject line read, "Can you verify sources?" and another, "Are you in possession of supporting documents?" How I wanted to read these e-mails. It was the first time one of my articles had received such a response, but time was short. I collected copies of the broadcast-quality video the compound had produced, a nice compilation of sound bites followed by an interview featuring Daniel Rami and Yoshi. Arturo had sent dozens of these to newsrooms, but I wanted the extras in case the media personnel who showed up had misplaced theirs.

Satisfied, I left the bunker, knowing that Abe Fritz was still in his office, perhaps calling a few low-level government workers who were, what he called, in his hip pocket. Outside the evening air was cool; sulfur-filled lamps gave the ground a pleasant tangerine glow. For a moment I wondered how we must look to the federal agents who, no doubt, were watching our every move through high-powered telescopes. I wondered if the media was already there, camped out in their production vans, satellite dishes raised. I wondered, too, if my father had seen me yet, his son, standing in the center of the compound holding a box of videotapes, a small man whose image moved across his TV set.

I helped Daniel secure the front entrance, looping a length of chain through the gate then snapping the lock home. He explained that we didn't want to be *too* secure because that could be dangerous. Then we attached a wooden sign to the kiosk that read "Private Property, The Dalai Yoshi Compound" in letters large enough to be videotaped from over a mile away. When I asked why Daniel kept checking the sky, he said, "Standard ATF procedure. Send in helicopters to distract the compound from an eminent ground assault."

"See any?"

"Not yet," he said.

I walked back to the Olive Branch Bunker believing we might be in for a good two- or three-day standoff, an event that would arouse significant media interest, but something seemed out of place. Where were the military transport vehicles? The raid crew in camouflage? The government-owned PA system issuing demands interspersed with loud rock music designed to wear down our resolve? I looked at the lonely Texas foothills, nothing more than black curves against a charcoal sky. There was movement there, three pairs of headlights aimed in our direction.

Feeling I'd done all I could, I returned to Yoshi's private altar, where he prayed with the advanced followers while a CD player produced the "Music of Bells and Finger Cymbals." For the first time I understood the importance of this music: it amplified the rhythms of the world so completely that I lost sight of all my usual distractions. I no longer thought of my father or law school or even jokes I liked on *Seinfeld*. I was centered in myself, thinking only of how I might do good in the world.

By this time, Yoshi had stopped praying and was spending a few moments beside each of his advanced followers, kneeling and doing breathing exercises. When he came to me, the lowliest in the bunch, I saw how he looked at my arm curiously out of the side of his eyes. After he kneeled, I thought I'd have to do the breathing exercises, only I wasn't quite sure how to do them. Instead he said, "You are good to be here. The other workers all left."

"They weren't followers yet," I told him.

"But you—you have dreams. This I already know."

"I dream about being in the desert. With this old man who gave me his tablets."

"Moses," he explained.

"We eat bread off the ground."

"He gives you the law. You must carry it. You might be one of the secret teachers."

"I am only a lawyer and a PR man. I don't know how to teach."

"Sometimes the teachers are a secret even to themselves." Through the chapel window we saw a yellow light alerting us to a possible raid, but Yoshi stayed with me, his hand on my elbow even as the advanced followers left the room. "Do you know why God works through the humble?"

"No," I said.

"Because the proud like to take all the credit for themselves."

With this he returned to his own pillow, centered before the candles where he did his prayers and breathing exercises. I understood I could leave if I wanted, but I stayed, trying my best to do the breathing exercises with him. Though I heard cars entering the compound, I pictured myself inside a protective bubble of polycarbonate glass where no one could bother me. Just when I was beginning to experience the cleansing quality of air, two advanced followers lifted Yoshi from his pillow and guided him out the door. Before they left, one looked back, his face screwed up in confusion as though there was something wrong with me to stay so long while the compound was under siege.

Outside I expected to find pandemonium but instead found four late-model Tauruses along with two sheriff's cars and a small Ryder truck, all of them pulled up to the main office, its thick door already jimmied. Most of Yoshi's followers were doing a fabulous job. Five or six young men walked about in pre-ripped T-shirts, while Mona Dischell captured the moment on video. Across the compound Darin Jacobs used a megaphone to alert whoever might be out there that we were a peaceful, nonviolent order who sought world harmony. Maya Anderson, assistant cook, unrolled a banner from a second-story window that called Yoshi a "Prophet for our Time."

I kept looking for federal agents brandishing high-caliber rifles. Instead I found three local deputies standing guard while a group of middle-aged men loaded computers and filing cabinets into the Ryder truck. How strange this raid, so unlike the training videos in which federal agents arrived in cattle trucks so as not to give themselves away.

I was about to push through a group of new converts, curiously milling about in their novice robes and gas masks, when Abe Fritz found me, his face pinched with anger, his shirt unbuttoned at the collar. I didn't know why he was so upset. At least we had federal agents here, hopefully media as well, but when I told him this, he only grew more irate. "These aren't ATF agents, you moron. This is the IRS. This is the State Department of Gambling. You told the whole fucking world we're running an online casino."

He was about to hit me, but Daniel Rami caught his arm, then shot him a look of urgency before leading him to the exercise area, where Yoshi was being pushed into the back of our Humvee.

Remembering my mission, I fought through the crowd. I expected to see agents with video cameras and beyond the gate representatives from local affiliates, but no one was there except for one rather severe-looking man dressed in a yellow windbreaker, the back of which read "Texas Department of Public Safety." When he made a move to confiscate my videotapes, I ran. I was tackled before I reached the road, plastic handcuffs closed around my wrists. I lay there, the officer's knee pressed into my back as our Humvee pulled out of the compound, Yoshi looking at me through the back window, his face holding great pity and great peace.

¤

Needless to say my trial was a quick one. I was brought up on charges of illegal casino operation, racketeering, and resisting arrest. My court-appointed attorney, Robert Jones, himself a graduate of Northeast Arroyo State, seemed to think I was screwed from the get-go. "By your own admission—in those articles you wrote—you helped compose the casino newsletter." After my coworkers were added to the witness list, I believed the jury might finally know my role at the compound was that of media relations/attorney, but on the stand, under the watchful eye of Abe Fritz's brother, they claimed "attorney-client privilege." Even Tami, my last hope, was unable to help. As she left the witness box, I saw a trace of regret in her eyes, a sadness she tried to hide by putting on a pair of sunglasses. None of them stayed long enough to hear the verdict: two counts of accessory.

This brings me to where I am now, serving twenty-two months at a minimum-security prison outside Dallas. Occasionally I send letters to Tami as a way of encouraging her Cherubic promptings. In my dreams I return to the desert, where Moses continually demands his tablets back. After seven months I'm no longer homesick, except when I see Corporate Sano trucks heading to a new facility they've opened just up the road.

In truth I've made a go of it here, working in the laundry and as the proofreader/editor for Robert Mahoney, a fellow convict who held public office in Houston and is now writing his memoir. I try to be open with everyone I meet, explaining as much of Yoshi's message as I understand, particularly the part about how necessary it is to turn away from selfishness. Surprisingly Robert and his friends have been very receptive. They're all important members of the Republican Party, doing time for a misunderstanding about land investments. They're under the impression a tax cut would be the best way to motivate people toward change, such as a big tax cut for hiring quotas and meeting outdated environmental standards that will probably be overturned anyway.

At first I thought they were pulling my leg about a career in politics, but after they introduced me to party officials during visiting days, I saw their intent. They know of a district outside San Antonio where I might be a shoo-in for state representative—a district that wouldn't hold my conviction against me and might even see it as a plus. Officially I'd run with the popular "Complete Tax Reform" branch of the Texas Republican Party, but once in office I'd have some leeway to help write laws I felt were important as well.

At dusk, as I walk along the perimeter of our prison's putting range, I often think about my future while looking for methane rainbows arched above the foothills. I believe I might be useful as a politician, one who is not only committed to Complete Tax Reform but also to improving human life. I might enact a significant tax cut for individuals who volunteer with troubled teens. Traffic tickets could be forgiven for spending a weekend building houses for the poor.

I don't expect my ideas to be popular, at least not at first. People resist their Cherubic nature, but Yoshi often said "Feelings follow action." So as the people of Texas learn to treat each other better, compelled by tax cuts and legal incentives, they may feel better about themselves, so much so they'll continue to act this way on their own accord. And after Texas improves, I'll take my ideas to other states, where I know I'll be met with ridicule and scorn. But I'll try not to let it bother me because deep down I'll know I am doing what is most important, spreading Yoshi's message, trying to thicken the supply of Cherubic blood in the world, even if I am able only to thicken that supply by a little.

Sirens

Still I think about her. Jackie Stevens, a fellow grad student. Jackie, with shoulder-length rust hair, high cheekbones, and large eyes that gave the impression she was slightly disappointed in the world no matter how good things got. She was in the theater department, while I was in English. One might think we'd have a number of classes together, but we only had one, Renaissance Drama, which I took to satisfy my Pre-Eighteenth-Century Brit Lit requirement.

She sat on the opposite side of the room, near Dr. Hobson, our seminar director, and rarely looked my way, though I was aware of her, as were most men in the course. She came to class wearing tank tops and jeans, her hair pulled back into a French braid, and took occasional notes while Old Hobson rattled on about the social merits of Jacobean drama. From other students, I knew she was a part-time catalog model and that she'd stopped dating men at the university, though she occasionally went out with a lawyer or a bank officer, both of whom seemed out of my league. Because of this, I was surprised, a year later, when she started talking to me at a student photography exhibition.

I saw her walk in, escorted by two or three people attached to the photography department. She wore a black cocktail dress, complete with pumps and smoke nylons, and appeared genuinely interested in my friend Bob's work. At the time, Bob was into large-format photography. His current series focused on modern adaptations of Greek myths. In one photo, entitled "Narcissus," a teenage girl dressed in a torn evening gown looked at her reflection in a community pool. In another, "Medusa," a young man held up a mirror to an old woman with skin haggard from years of smoking. I was doing my best to mix in, say hello to anyone I knew and dodge any guilt-provoking questions about my dissertation, which I had yet to start.

When I could take no more, I waved to Bob, who was chatting up a local art dealer, and went to the balcony to have a smoke. In truth, I was only an occasional smoker and trying to quit. Since finishing my coursework I'd had a lot of free time on my hands, and one of the things I'd learned was this: I was not the best with free time. I worked much more efficiently on a regular schedule, and though I still taught one freshman course each term, it wasn't enough to direct my life toward productive research and eventual writing. I'd spent a number of nights playing poker with the guys. During these card games, I'd also eaten a lot of Cheetos, so much so I'd put on ten pounds. Because of this, I'd spent a number of afternoons playing basketball in an attempt to lose this weight, though most of these afternoons degenerated into evening card games and consequently more Cheetos. What these days did not yield was honest research, and though I was relatively certain no one, including my own committee, would ever read much of my dissertation, I still needed one to graduate.

By the time I'd finished my cigarette I was somewhat pleased with myself because I'd thrown the rest of the pack over the balcony and into the bushes, along with my lighter and two dollars I'd forgotten I'd rolled into the pack until I'd let the thing fly. I ordered a couple more drinks, drank them, and was talking to Buster Thompson, a grad student in history, when Jackie came over to see us. We talked about school for a while and then modeling—as it turned out Buster did some modeling on the side—and when he left, I was surprised she stayed and talked to me. She told me she wanted to be in stage productions and didn't particularly like modeling. I told her that when I was a kid, I'd wanted to work with movies. "I didn't want to be in them," I clarified, "just do things, like casting or post-production."

"What are you going to do now?" she asked.

"Magazine work if I can get it," I said. "I'd like to teach, but I just don't see myself getting a job right away."

"I'm still doing catalog work," she said. "It keeps me away from waitressing and frees up my days for other things."

"Can't you get a teaching assistantship in your department?"

"I could," she said, "but I'm thinking about dropping out. I think I've learned all I needed to learn in grad school."

I knew this wasn't true for me: I'd come to grad school hoping that a more confident, knowledgeable version of myself would emerge. Instead, I'd discovered I was the same person I'd always been. Sure, I knew a lot of facts. I could do a few neat tricks, like whip any essay into MLA format at the drop of a hat, but aside from that I hadn't grown in the ways I'd expected. We talked until the exhibit lights went out, and only then did we realize we'd talked for almost two hours, our drinks gone, the ice mostly melted.

We walked to the parking lot, where, beneath sulfur-filled street lamps, we saw our cars. Ironically, they were parked side by side, as though we were destined to be paired this evening. I placed my hand on her hip. She turned to me, a willingness in her eyes, and I kissed her, slowly at first, my lips open only a little. Then she said the oddest thing: "You're braver than you were in class."

"I've been drinking," I said.

I kissed her again, more deliberately this time. I circled my arms around her waist, my hands high on her back, and when we'd been kissing for a minute or two, I began to stroke the side of her breast with my thumb. I was a little drunk, yet very attracted to her. I liked her voice. I liked her eyes and how, right then, her leg was moving against my groin. By now, my hands were cupping her breasts, and when we started kissing again she looked meaningfully toward my car.

Once inside it, I held her bare breasts in my hands, surprisingly full breasts for a catalog model, then kissed them until her nipples began to swell. I traced the outline of her body, from her chin to her navel, and while I did, she undid my belt and then my jeans. "Can you come while you're drunk?" she asked.

"I don't see it being a problem," I said.

With her fingers ringed around my erection, she lowered her mouth over me, moving her tongue in long, slow turns, until I felt a rhythm between us. I ran my fingers through her hair and down her back, and just as I did, who did I see? Who else but Bob, leaving the exhibition hall, a small manila folder under his arm. He looked a little sad and dejected, which meant the dealer had shrugged him off, but he seemed to perk up when he saw me. I made certain hand motions to him, such as emphatically pointing at my lap, where Jackie moved and twisted. All the while, I made encouraging sounds because I wanted her to know I was interested. I groaned and said, "Oh, that feels good" and, "Yes, there." Only when she took a break, lifting herself to kiss me, did she see Bob, still fifteen feet from my car. Only then did Bob understand my cryptic gestures. He stood there, the jaundiced light all around him, his mouth open. "Oh Bob," she groaned.

"You know him?" I asked.

"I did some work with him," she said, then stuck her head out the window. "Professional favor, Bob," she said.

"Get lost?" he asked.

"That's the one," she said, then turned to me, passion still evident in her eyes, and said, "Now where were we?"

"Blow job," I replied, "halfway through."

"Halfway?" she said. "Unless I'm wrong, we're just getting started."

We stayed in my car fifteen minutes, then drove to her apartment, a small one-bedroom unit on the peninsula. We made love slowly on her bed, with her cat watching us from the bookshelf, and when we finished we fell asleep to the sound of hushed waves in the distance. I woke two or three times, startled to find myself in someone else's bed, moonlight slanting in around us. She looked very pretty lying beside me, the sheet tucked around her shoulders, her eyes pinched shut, her mouth slightly open. She took slow, deep breaths, her chest expanding then contracting.

Toward morning, I thought I might get up, perhaps take a gander at the sea, but just as I was about to, I turned to her. There was something about her—how she brought her eyebrows together, I think—which led me to believe she was not as confident or as secure as she let on. Rather, she was scared of the big world, just like I was, and not quite sure what to do with herself. I stayed with her another half hour, my hand on her shoulder, but when the sun entered the room, I rose and made coffee.

A half hour later she walked out to the kitchen, wearing a terrycloth robe. I was sitting in her breakfast nook, looking out at early morning surfers, their boards dotting the water like debris. She sat across from me and after giving me the once-over, said, "I hope you don't feel weird about last night."

"I don't feel weird about it," I said.

"Good," she replied. "I don't want you to."

I touched her arm, right where the robe cuffed it, then handed her my cup. "Take this," I offered. "I'll get another for myself."

I left her apartment feeling surprisingly good. Though I considered going home, taking some aspirin, and having a good long nap, I only went there to take a shower and check in with my roommate, Baxter, who was a computer science student. Even though he wouldn't defend his dissertation for another year, he already had three job offers. When he wasn't working on research he spent a good deal of time designing web pages for cash. "You out playing cards last night?" he asked, glancing up from his computer screen.

"Not exactly," I said.

"Oh," he noted, but he was too interested in other things to ask where I'd been.

I went to the library, as I did a few times a week, and read articles for my dissertation. Initially I'd been interested in gender roles in American fiction—male rituals, to be exact—but after coming here for the last six months, I was now hoping some other people had done most of the work, had developed interesting theories, and that all I'd have to do was collect them, cite a million sources, and spew the whole mess out in proper dissertation format. I worked until four, scribbling down a few nifty ideas, and on my way out I stopped by periodicals and looked at the addresses of magazines I liked.

That night at Bob's house we played cards, as per our usual routine. I arrived late, sans Cheetos, though Larry had an extra-large bag already open, another in reserve. The room was dim, the tequila on the counter, the vague aroma of pot in the air though no one had yet lit up. I sat in my usual spot, beside Albert, then took out a large baggie in which I kept my poker change and set it on the table, before I realized that half the guys were eyeing me. I popped open a beer, took a sip, then turned to Bob, who sat at the head of the table. "Thanks, Bob," I said.

"English Boy," Larry said, "he gets a knob job."

"So what happened?" Albert asked.

"No details," I said.

"No details?" Bob repeated. "Was she totally nude when I saw her in your car?"

"No," I said. "She was not totally nude."

"English Boy," Larry said, "giving up the details."

"Cards," I said, dealing a few off the deck. I gave everyone my best pissed-off look, and only then did I understand that I had actual feelings for Jackie. "Five-card draw," I said, "deuces and one-eyeds wild."

¤

In the weeks that followed I spent a good deal of time with Jackie. At first we saw each other only on weekends but eventually on weekdays as well. I'd drive to her house, usually around six, and we'd make dinner together, something simple like pasta, and afterwards we'd either walk on the beach or lie around her apartment. Initially we made love often. She had a thin, agile body and enjoyed variations on the missionary position. Often she placed a pillow under her back so her hips arched and our bodies met at a slightly sharper angle. After sex, we would lie on the floor, a blue fleece blanket beneath us, and read stories to each other or eat raw vegetables or fruit. When we did retire to bed, I noticed that same nocturnal transformation—her daytime self melting away, small worry lines gracing her face. I became convinced that, like me, she did not know what to do with her life and was afraid the world would damage her in some unforeseen way.

A few days later, I brought window locks to her apartment, a whole bag of them, and while she was making dinner, I installed them on her downstairs windows, twisting the miniature C-clamps into place. She did not notice right away—she was telling me about some letch at a photo shoot—but after dinner, she warmed to me in a way she hadn't before. She sat on the couch with me watching *Jeopardy!*, her legs tucked under her, but afterward she examined my handiwork, the tiny silver latches attached to the metal guides. "It's not quite a dozen roses," I said, then placed my hand on her shoulder. I saw a glimpse of that other nighttime person, the woman who acknowledged some small fear of the world. I felt she was letting me see this as a reward for understanding her, but by the time we'd washed the dishes, this other person had left us, retreating until her body was fast asleep.

I soon became accustomed to the two Jackies—the daytime model and the one I glimpsed at home. When we went out I was constantly aware of how men looked at her, quick sideways glances. Once, at an Italian restaurant, our waiter left his number on the bill. Another time, at a bar, a man asked me if I was her brother or something. She was quite good with men. She never led them on, yet in spite of this, they gave her things. Phil at One-Hour Photo developed her film for free, the guys at Baskin-Robbins gave her free ice cream, and as for the men at the car wash, you'd be surprised what they did. I mean, her car sparkled.

She liked being pretty. She liked how people treated her. At catalog shoots she'd kiss the photographer, usually on the cheek though sometimes lightly on the lips, then sit while a girl slightly less beautiful applied makeup to her eyes, cheeks, and lips before she dressed in that week's designer duds and posed. Because it was early spring, she spent a good deal of time modeling the following fall's sweaters and wool pants—she had the right body for sweaters, she once told me—and after the shoot was finished a security guard would escort her to her car because once, a few years ago, one of the girls had been assaulted in a parking lot.

When she returned home, she held the glow of her model personality, the beautiful woman she was in the world, and yet I could tell she wanted to leave part of this life behind, peel it off like one of the many sweaters she'd worn. Often she would find me at her kitchen table reading—since meeting her I studied more regularly—and then over tea she'd tell me about her day, until she said something like, "You want to have sex?" Then we'd lay the blue fleece blanket over the living room rug and arrange the pillows. After undressing, we'd make love, her hips arched as always, the two of us moving together, as though this were the means by which she became this other person, the private woman I was slowly coming to know and love.

As we lay there, she'd tell me about her life. She'd grown up in Mendocino. Her mother was a secretary, her father a hotel maintenance worker. Her one big dream was to move to the city and understand life there. Early on her mother wanted her to be a model, entering her in the occasional childhood beauty contest, believing that this would be a way for her to overcome her heritage, that of a second-generation Irish immigrant. She did not like modeling at first, though when strapped for cash as an undergrad she took to it again and found it an easy way to make money. "But honestly," she told me, "I'd rather work in theater."

"Why don't you?" I asked.

"It's a hard business to get into," she said, "and I don't have anyone to fall back on."

"You have me," I said.

But to this, she only smiled.

I continued with my school life—the library, my one section of freshman comp, the poker games at Bob's—but I felt removed from my old ways. With the exception of two or three lapses, I'd given up smoking entirely; I'd lost five pounds without really trying. More amazing, I'd typed eighty actual pages toward my dissertation, a feat so unexpected that when presented with them my major professor said, "You may graduate yet." Along with this, I was winning at poker. Since meeting Jackie, I found I could bluff more effectively. The other guys usually believed I had good cards when, in fact, I had junk, a pair at best, and would concede the pot to me.

After one of these poker games, I stayed at Bob's house, trying to sober up before walking home. I liked being with him because unlike most grad students at my school he had a sense about himself, a strong belief he would make it in his chosen field, which was something I had yet to cultivate. Since his student exhibition he'd had work accepted for a photography journal and was getting interest from New York about his modern myth series. "I need one more good shot," he confided, "and I think these feelers in the city will pan out. I want to do 'The Sirens.'"

I lay on the couch, opposite him. "What's 'The Sirens'?" I asked.

"Three women on a beach," he said. "I can swipe some fairly nice gowns from this guy I know. And in the foreground, a sailor. I want to overexpose it a little."

"Nice," I said.

"I've still got some student loan money," he said. "If my car doesn't break down, I think I can do the shot." He offered me more tequila, which I refused. "I figured you for the sailor."

"I'm no model," I said.

To this, he didn't respond. He just lay there, a rocks glass balanced on his chest. "Speaking of models," he said, "how's things with Jackie?"

"Good," I said.

"A lot of guys tried to go out with her before you."

"They probably all treated her as a model."

"Probably did," he said. "Sure you don't want another?" He waggled the bottle.

"I'm trying to sober up," I said. "Otherwise I'll be here all night."

¤

In the weeks that followed Jackie and I had a quiet, private life. At home she wore sweats and T-shirts. She would do things that surprised me, like bust out in a perfect, sarcastic imitation of our old teacher, Mr. Hobson, or talk back to the TV, berating Alex Trebek of *Jeopardy!* when he belittled a contestant. Sometimes she would sing softly while we did the dishes, and in these moments, I realized that she was falling in love with me, crooning an Irish lullaby that her mother once sang to her.

I was surprised how little people knew about her. Even her friends were content believing she was merely the model, a woman whose picture appeared in specialty catalogs like The Eddie Bauer Collection. They imagined her as a woman from a large, cosmopolitan city, San Francisco perhaps, who had grown up in an upper-middle-class family—a girl of privilege who had been taken to Paris as a child, sent off to private schools, though none of that was true. For the most part her friends discussed modeling or films or different exercise programs they were trying. Only at night, after she had been with me a while, would she soften to this other person, this woman who had once wanted to study theater, who worried that her parents would die young and who occasionally read eighteenth-century English poetry because she found it beautiful and difficult to understand.

In general, I was pleased with my life. I'd finished 155 pages of my dissertation. Except for the occasional joint, I didn't smoke at all. More importantly, I was wearing jeans I'd owned when I started grad school, size 33s that were faded and worn at the knees, their pockets stained from green highlighters I used to carry to my first literature seminar. Even the poker guys noticed the change. One night after we were all a little stoned, Larry started in on his English Boy lines again. "English Boy," he said, "he falls in love. He bets brazenly. He fleeces his friends at poker night."

"I have not fleeced anyone," I said.

"English Boy," he said, "he fleeces his friends then lies about it."

But I didn't say anything because he was partly right; I often left the table with a few extra dollars. For the first time in my adult life, I was content and a little surprised to find this emotion in me. Larry dealt a new hand, two of my first three cards aces, then called the game. "Chicago baseball," he said.

¤

The tragedy occurred in July—July 7, to be precise—shortly after Jackie left a catalog shoot. Jake Lewis, an off-duty policeman, walked her to her car as he had many other days, and later that evening, after the swimsuit models finished, he walked two other girls to their cars, including Jackie's friend, Trisha Wells. According to Jake, Trish was okay when he last saw her, sitting in the driver's seat, looking for an R.E.M. tape. Sometime before she found it—before she'd even started the engine—another person, most likely a man, entered her car and strangled her, using braided electrical wire attached to triangular handles. Her body was found the next day, stuffed into her own trunk. The car was abandoned at a beach two miles from where Jackie lived.

Following Trish's death, Jackie stayed home, all the doors locked, and watched self-defense videos produced especially for models. As she watched them she seemed to be thinking about other things, her eyes focused on some imaginary object located miles outside her apartment. I brought her dinner, Thai peanut noodles, one of her favorite dishes, and when she felt like eating, she picked at them with the wooden chopsticks included in the takeout bag. "She was really pretty," she said. "She could've done magazines. She just had that look." Using her chopsticks, she tweezed a few noodles to her mouth. "Do you think beautiful people are cursed? I mean, they're blessed in certain ways, but do you think they're cursed as well?"

"Not really," I said. "It was just some sicko who had a thing for her."

"I'm fairly sure of this," she said. "If Trish weren't pretty—you know, if she were just a little plain—she'd still be alive today."

Later that night we made love on the couch, and even when we moved to the floor, the blanket beneath us, she did not use the pillows like she usually did. Instead we lay side by side, one of her legs hooked over me, and after that she asked to make love sitting up, which was something we'd never done before. She controlled the pace, and when she closed her eyes, she seemed to forget herself. Her whole body focused on this act, twisting and bending, pushing in ways I tried to follow. Exhausted, we went to bed early, but she was not the person she usually was with me. She did not talk about her parents or touring productions she wanted to see or even about poetry she liked. She simply fell asleep, her body folded away from mine, my hand on her arm, her skin cool and smooth.

Away from the house she wore large smoky glasses and summer jackets that covered her body. Sometimes she tied a scarf around her hair. She blended into crowds and, except for photo developing, no longer received free goods and services. Twice, on our evening walks, we went to the beach where Trish's car had been discovered, the side window cracked, a woman's fingernail embedded into the dash, and each time, Jackie stood there, her arms slightly extended. "You know," she said, "my mom was only able to see the glamorous side of modeling. She thought it was so much better than the life she had."

I moved beside her. I understood something about her, from the way her eyes were fixed on low, sunburnt clouds. She was thinking about what it meant to have her own life and what possibilities remained open to her. When the sky turned gray, I suggested we go home. That night, we made Top Ramen—a poor substitute for Thai noodles—and ate them in front of the TV. After *Jeopardy!* we kissed on the sofa, soft dating kisses we had not exchanged in a long time. Eventually she unbuttoned my shirt and kissed my chest, then began with my belt, but once, as she looked up, I saw only a vague recognition, a momentary forgetfulness, as though for a split second she did not know who I was or what I was doing there. I put it down to grief—or rather, some general confusion brought on by grief—and that night in bed I hummed a simple tune she had taught me, one of her mother's Irish lullabies, as car lights from outside moved across the walls.

In the days that followed, she bought books about changing careers; she ordered brochures about fellowships in drama. During a conversation about New York, she finally told her girlfriends she was the daughter of Irish immigrants in Mendocino, and when they looked at her a little cockeyed, she simply said, "Small town girl makes good," at which they laughed. We no longer made love on the blue fleece blanket, and the following Sunday when I joined her in the shower, she looked at me a little surprised, her eyes sad for some reason, but then turned around and I scrubbed her back as usual.

Two days later I found a tan Mercedes parked in her visitor's space, a cardboard screen unfolded across its dash. I parked across the street, near the sand dunes. I sat in my car, already understanding, and when I finally got out, I saw Jackie through her upstairs window, the Venetian blinds partly closed. She stood there, wearing a green tank top, her hair pulled up into a French braid, much like it had been when I met her. She tucked stray strands behind her ear. She touched her chin while talking. She smiled, revealing a certain coyness I'd always suspected was in her, but had never seen. Here she was, this other Jackie, the one who worried about her parents and read poetry, her expressions more fully revealed. Here she was, the woman she mostly hid from the world and still half-hid from me, the one I so much wanted to know and love.

At first I could not move, but simply sat on my hood watching. They talked, looked at some book, then he kissed her, this man who upon seeing him I knew was one of her previous boyfriends, dressed in a thin blue blazer, white shirt, no tie—a tall man, his hair neatly parted, a banker or a lawyer. I did not need to be told the obvious, that I wasn't the first to find this hidden part of Jackie, though in my earlier, self-deluded state I fancied I was. There were other men undoubtedly who had not seen her as the model, other men who had riddled out the secrets of her soul, and sitting there, I understood I wasn't even the best of them. The proof was above me, fixed behind a bedroom window. Their bodies touched, as did their lips, and when they moved toward the bed I felt so mad and empty I picked up a big dirt clod and flung it at his car, its form exploding against the fender and leaving dust across the hood. I threw another, this time setting off his car alarm. Amidst the bells and sirens she came to the window, parted two slats and saw me there, across the street, near the beach that had been, until that day, our favorite place to walk. Her eyes widened, then she made her way to the front door, but before she got there, I was already gunning the engine, so that by the time she came outside, wearing nothing more than a tank top and shorts, I was up the street, fishtailing onto the highway.

I went home, relieved to have the place to myself, and sat on my bed, my books stacked around me. "Fuck, fuck, fuck, fuck, fuck," I said, then I pounded my hand against the wall. "Fuck," I said again then I went outside, where the sun was still bright across our apartment lawn. I walked from the community mailboxes to the 7-11 three times before finally sitting at a bus stop. Three buses came. I waved each on before walking back to my apartment to check my messages. The tape was empty.

¤

I was determined not to call her. I wanted to live in my own world, be satisfied with my own friends, but at night I pictured her beside me, covered in a thin percale sheet, her hair held back with bobby pins, but when I rolled to see her, I found my backpack or the extra pillows stacked at the edge of the bed. Each morning I woke, I showered, I made myself eat something, if only a slice of toast, then went to the library. I tried to read but found my eyes skimming words while I thought of Jackie. I forced myself to stay there, productive or not, until four-thirty, though I took a lot of breaks that ended up lasting an hour or so.

On these breaks, I walked through campus, tall eucalyptus trees arching over me, freshmen sunning themselves near their dorms. I followed the crisscrossing trails to the science complex and back, often stopping at the student union for coffee or jellybeans. I wanted cigarettes so bad I could taste them. Twice I bought packs of Camels and twice I tossed them out. I chastised myself for being so stupid, so weak, then I went back to the library to fake-read some more, hoping I would look up and magically the clock would have advanced to four-thirty.

That Saturday I received her letter. In it, she told me that she didn't want to hurt me, that she loved me but was confused. "Sometimes," she said, "I'm not even sure who I am or what I need." And then she told me about the man, an old boyfriend she'd left a few years ago, a man who had recently lost his parents in a car accident, a soft man, she explained, who was a lot like her. "I didn't think I needed him," she said, "but I guess I did." She asked me to call her, underlining the words, but I just set the letter on my desk beside a stack of bills, then did some deep breathing on the balcony.

Not long after that, I received a few calls that on the machine registered as hang-ups, and after that, I received one message, her voice choked, asking me to call. But I didn't want to break down and tell her how much I loved her, how bad I was hurting. I didn't want to say those words and own up to all the ways I missed her, and so after listening to her message for five days, I put a new tape into the machine and placed the old one in a drawer.

I was determined to be the conscientious, work-oriented person I'd been while I was with her. I kept my schedule at the library. I forced myself to write. Every second week I submitted new pages to my major professor, who reviewed them with guarded optimism. Surprisingly, I was starting to get a little magazine work as well. *Buzz* called me to do a restaurant review. *Details* asked for a short piece on men's boxers. I thought some of Bob's confidence was starting to rub off on me. As for Jackie, I learned she'd stopped seeing that man and, through friends, knew she missed me as well. Late at night, I considered calling but never did.

☒

By genial cajoling Bob convinced me to be his sailor, posed before a trio of girls all decked out in lacy white numbers he nicked from a job he did uptown. I went with him to rent equipment, and while in the camera shop he decided not to rent two pieces he'd hoped to use. "Photography on a budget," he said. We got my outfit from the drama department, a faded leather vest and poet's shirt, and on the day of the shoot, I was surprised how much I looked like a sailor. As he'd requested, I didn't comb my hair, but let it dry au naturel to give the impression I'd recently washed ashore.

I parked at the end of the dirt lot and when I got out I found Bob leaning against his van, his arms crossed, gazing down at the beach. Together we looked at the site, a small private beach surrounded by cliffs. Already he'd set up the equipment, and just then his assistant, Rooski, was adjusting a flash screen while a makeup girl dusted the models with face powder. "We have a problem," he said. I turned to him, noticing his pale face, his half-closed eyes. "I requested three specific girls, but one was sick, so the agency sent a replacement."

Only then did I look at the girls more carefully. At the far end, near three folding chairs, I saw Jackie, her hair shorter, her body thinner than I remembered. She stood there, oblivious of me, wearing a strapless evening gown and long white gloves. "Does she know I'm here?"

"She thinks she can do it," he said, then put his hand on my arm. "I called the agency, but they're closed for the day. I wouldn't ask you to do it," he said, his eyes meeting mine, "but I've spent the last of my student loan money, and my credit cards are tapped out. I don't have the funds to redo this another day."

I looked at the girls standing there, their feet bare, their eyes already accented with color, and after I saw Jackie again, my stomach began to hurt. "I can do this," I said. "Give us a few minutes to talk."

"Sure," he said. "You have no idea what this means to me."

I followed the slender dirt trail, sided by overgrown coastal shrubs, until I reached the beach, my feet moving thickly through the sand. I was trying to approach the situation with a certain grace, but when she held me in her gaze I simply froze, unable to move, my heart thumping away in my chest.

I met her halfway, near the chalky cliffs, and once there, I saw she was upset, too. She kept clasping and unclasping her hands. Her eyes, already a little damp, looked off at the sea. We didn't really know how to greet each other and settled on hello. I felt so awkward standing beside her, unable to touch or kiss her. She said she was doing well, that she'd been working a lot. "I didn't mean to mess everything up so bad," she said.

"I should've called," I said.

She dabbed at a tear and smeared makeup on her glove. She was close to crying, as was I. "I was hoping it wouldn't be so hard," she said, then touched her eye again, only to find that her glove held another spot of makeup. "Shit," she said, "shit."

At this, Rooski walked over to us, a light meter in his hand. "Why don't you do the shoot first?" he suggested. "Talk afterwards."

I watched as she rejoined the other girls, her body half composing itself into the model persona she was so good at projecting into the world, though she was unable to fit inside this role right then, her face betraying a sense of sadness or regret.

By now, Bob was a little excited, taken again with his project, as the sun lowered itself toward the horizon, giving off its magic evening light.

Above us a few clouds streaked the sky, and when he noticed them, he said, "Perfect. Just perfect. The hint of a storm recently passed." He arranged the girls first, clustering the other two around Jackie, since she was the tallest, and directed them to stretch out their arms in such a way as to mock-invite men to their shore. Eventually he placed me before them, kneeling in the sand. I saw Jackie trying so hard to present her familiar model's eyes, her model's mouth, her face holding only the emotions appropriate for this shoot, but in them, I saw a certain longing and confusion; I'd like to say sorrow but don't know if that was there or not.

"OK, girls," Bob said, "you know what to do." Then to me, he said, "One hand raised, old buddy, almost touching theirs."

I raised my hand and tried to become that sailor washed ashore, drawn by the voices of women I could not resist, the models before me decked out in high-end evening wear, one with a prom corsage looped around her wrist. I looked at Jackie, her arms beckoning me, her body like that ancient temptress, though her eyes revealed pure longing, as did mine. I wanted so badly to touch her, to hold her, to let our lips meet, but already sensed these things would never happen. We would never again kiss, never lie on her couch watching *Jeopardy!*, never again make love on her fleece blanket, a pillow positioned under her back. We would never again have any of that relationship, though at that moment I wanted it all back. After the shoot we would sit in her car. Again she'd tell me she was sorry. She was going back to school, she'd say. I'd tell her about my magazine work, about my coming graduation, that I was sorry, too, but we wouldn't find the language to reclaim our love. On the beach, though, I simply looked at her as Bob snapped shot after shot, already believing these prints would launch his career in New York. "Perfect," he said, "perfect."

She stood there, inviting me with her arms, her body taking on a hint of eroticism attributed to the mythic sirens as the clouds purpled above her. I watched this girl I once loved, sensing I'd never have her again and allowing those feelings to wash over me, a thick coppery sadness I'd never felt, and understood just then that my heart was broken—that it was in fact breaking—and hoped I was strong enough to accept this, though doubted I was, as my sailor hands reached for hers only to find that the distance was too far, too great, even after the shoot was finished and we walked to the car, still dressed in costume, to cry and talk and understand that all roads lead ahead and that our love was buried somewhere in the past.

Newsworld II

We watched it in Social Studies, then in World History. That Friday, September 14, we saw it again in a class called Life Studies. When the jet slammed into the north tower, Mr. Stolz, our teacher, squeezed the bridge of his nose pensively just like he did when he lectured about the dangers of credit-card debt. He shifted his eyes to us, his class of eleventh-grade boys, and asked how we felt about the attack.

We weren't good at talking about our feelings, though Mr. Stolz had made us read a book called *The Emotional Life of Men*. Our emotions were mysterious to us, the fine divisions between melancholy and depression, yearning and desire. We suspected that someday soon we'd be able to tell the difference between such things, the same way our parents could tell the difference between a good wine and a *very* good wine. We didn't tell Mr. Stolz much about our lives. For example, we didn't tell him that Jay Moore had videotaped the attack, then watched it after doing three lines of Ritalin. Nor did we tell him that Jeff Loeb's little brother, Seth, had laughed when he saw the first jet exploding into the tower. He'd thought it was a movie, like *Independence Day*. After his teacher explained that the planes were real, he cried for ten minutes before going to recess and kicking a red activity ball over the playground fence.

We sat quietly, waiting for Mr. Stolz to talk to us. From previous classes we'd learned there were special scripts for talking about your feelings. For example, there were specific things you should say to a friend with a serious drug problem. But we didn't know the script for this situation. Alan Whidden, a boy who'd been busted for steroids, said, "It makes me angry." Mr. Stolz stood there in his starched black T-shirt and ironed jeans, regarding us with stern eyes. Harry Kessel, a JV lineman, said, "We should get whoever did this."

We were scared, but didn't know how to say we were scared. The men in our textbook weren't the kind of men you saw in the suburbs of Atlanta. They weren't the kind who told their sons, "Kick some ass in the game this weekend" or, "If you're going to do it, for god's sake wear a rubber." Our fathers went fishing ten times a year and rode tractor mowers around our weedy suburban lawns. They hung punching bags in our garages, the nylon casings filled with the exact amount of sand to make the bags feel like dead bodies.

Initially we believed the terrorist attacks were something that happened up north, a good ways above the Mason-Dixon Line. But then our airport closed. The freeway closed, the mall closed, so did the movie theater. Lastly Newsworld draped a thick black chain across the entrance to its parking lot, right in front of the attendant booths where Jeff Sanders and Jarvis White had collected the five-dollar parking fee from tourists all summer long. A professionally printed sign announced, "National Security Closure."

Most of us worked at Newsworld, an amusement park three miles from our school. We said we hated it, but in truth we didn't mind it so much. We sold Icees and scraped gum off the sidewalk. We stole stuffed animals from the gift shops and gave them to our girlfriends. We thought the job was educational and believed it would help us get into a good college.

After my evening shift I liked to walk through the park. I particularly liked The Vietnam Experience, three acres so lush you forgot you were in central Georgia, a silver mist rising from vents hidden in rocks, water dripping from irrigation hoses molded to resemble jungle vines. It was kind of creepy, the way it was laid out, the huts made of sticks, military radios and grenade launchers left beside the Main Guest Trail. Sometimes I would meet my girlfriend, Devon MacCray, in the Lost Vietnamese Village. We would make out in one of the thatched huts while a cool breeze circled around us and the soft voices of the Vietcong whispered from miniature speakers hidden in banyan trees.

We'd grown up with Newsworld, the way other kids had grown up with Disney or Six Flags. Our parents had taken us there when we were seven or eight so we could walk through an authentic reproduction of a 1950s diner and sit behind the wheel of a 1955 Chevy Bel Air. We were made to watch a clumsy mannequin of Martin Luther King Jr. deliver highlights from his "I Have a Dream" speech while an equally clumsy mannequin of his wife quivered beside him.

We were ushered into the First Interactive Museum, a newsreel of our parents' lives spun out as entertainment. As children, we loved to ride the Kentucky Derby Carousel, control the U-Fly-Em Fighter Jets, watch Neil Armstrong step onto the moon, the gray lunar dust rising up around his opaque boot while we sat in a cozy reproduction of Mission Control, listening to the brassy fanfare of "The Star-Spangled Banner."

When we were teenagers we first experienced the strangeness of boarding a ride based on a news story we'd seen on TV. As little kids, we'd watched in irritation as OJ's Bronco crawled up the freeway followed by patrol cars and TV news helicopters, the live footage interrupting *Animaniacs* and *Duck Tales*. Five years later we climbed into similar Broncos—vehicles outfitted with lap bars and individual sound systems embedded into the headrests—and were whisked into the dim sound stage of Los Angeles. Dave Fowler, my best friend in junior high, told me, "This ride totally sucks." Yet we went on it three more times, until Doug could mimic the announcer's voice, a lazy California accent that made words such as "pursuit" sound more important than they did in the South.

We learned about the park's closure on September 11 while watching a team of reporters explore the wreckage of New York. A bulletin scrolled across the TV informing us that the park had been closed along with other public areas. My mother, a diet counselor for Jenny Craig, watched all day, clicking from one channel to the next. Each one showed the smoldering remains of the towers, surrounded by other buildings that experts believed would collapse as well. She ate saltines right out of the box, not from premeasured "snack baggies" she kept in the cupboard. "I shouldn't be eating these," she said, then put another one into her mouth.

Over the next two days, we drove by Newsworld many times, noting how odd it was to see the parking lot empty, how naked the sky appeared over the Titanic without artificial smoke rising from the cracked hull of the ship. Though signs warned against trespassing, we walked along the twelve-foot security fence that separated Newsworld from the rest of Georgia. Ron Watson, a boy who'd been arrested twice for shoplifting, was the first to throw stones. We listened as they landed inside the park, their sharp *pock-pock-pock* across the painted cement, then the enthusiastic hush of breaking glass.

We planned to break into the park on Saturday night, all of us wearing black shirts and jeans. We'd never been inside the park when it was closed. We'd never walked along Twentieth-Century Boulevard without hearing the cheerful calliope music that came from the snack wagon, nor had we seen the Boogie Nights Disco without pinwheels of colored lights spinning across the darkened front windows. Specifically we wanted to walk through an attraction called The San Francisco Earthquake, to stand among the crumpled buildings, the piles of bricks and metal covered by a fine, simulated dust. Though no one said as much, we felt we might better understand what had happened in New York if we could be inside the park for a while, on this street where buildings had been destroyed by a different tragedy.

We met at the delivery entrance, most of us half-drunk on schnapps. We were anxious yet sad. Sometimes we felt so many things we thought our bodies would burst. But other times we felt as though our hearts had been scraped out with a spoon. We were worried about the draft. Would there be a draft? We'd never been in love. We'd never done anything important, though our lives *felt* as important as a big summer movie.

We moved quietly into the park, sliding under a dusty gap in the fence. Lonnie Mason carried a flashlight he'd taken from his father's car, though no one allowed him to turn it on. Jimmy Kendral claimed to have the keys to the security shack, but when we tried them they didn't work. We walked down a street called Legends of the '50s, past diners just like those our grandparents had known—diners with over-stuffed red booths and jukebox menus at each table. We walked past the Daily Scoop, a gift shop where some of us had worked the previous summer. Dan Wheeler pressed his hands to the tinted glass so he could see inside; shadows fell across displays of news-related action figures, cash registers with their empty drawers left open, per the new employee guidelines.

Though we never said as much, we all felt the ragged ends of nostalgia brush against our hearts. Had we felt nostalgic before? Ron Watson missed his father who now lived across town. Jeff Loeb missed a girl who'd moved to Canada. But this was different. We ached to be fifteen again, to be washed in the silver colander of our sophomore year, a world of drivers' permits and diet-related acne. We longed to squeeze back into the snakeskin of our youth, to feel its safe snugness around our growing, muscular bodies.

We almost didn't recognize the park without the background music in each of its six themed lands. The Vietnam Experience looked like any other swamp. Where was the manufactured mist, the menacing chatter of the Vietcong? The large building that housed the OJ Simpson ride could have been any warehouse, without its signature neon sign and the image of OJ projected on a screen above the entrance.

We were disappointed because we saw how easily our childhood could be turned off, everything shut down and emptied. Behind an attraction called Hooverville, Jeff Loeb carved his initials into the soft pine exterior of a gift shop. Stephen Moore picked up a Visitors' Guide that listed the parade and show schedule for Monday, September 10. Karl Asher saw a quarter under a park bench and left it there.

We'd come here not knowing what to expect, though we all expected to learn something as we walked around the carefully organized debris of The San Francisco Earthquake, the piles of bricks, the broken pieces of plastic designed to look like glass. We wanted to feel something other than the vague ache we'd felt all week. We wanted emotion to fill our bodies like a golden light. Our teachers had told us the world would be different now—harder, difficult in ways we couldn't imagine.

Most of us had never been to New York. Our families had taken us on short vacations to New Orleans and Orlando, where we'd visited other theme parks, sometimes a zoo or a museum. Chuck Milligan, the only boy to fail his driving test, told us the Twin Towers were five times taller than any building in Atlanta. Though Chuck was prone to exaggeration, we tried to imagine the tallest building in Atlanta stacked on top of itself five times. We'd only seen the towers on TV, only noticed their impressive gray bulk as they fell to the ground in a burning, dusty heap. We were good at understanding TV. We knew some reality shows were more real than others, yet we didn't know how to feel about what we'd seen on September 11.

We were surprised that we didn't find security guards on Twentieth-Century Boulevard, yet relieved as well. We had a good sense about ourselves as we neared the far end of the park, a sense that we were not just marching through the unexamined life of the average boy at our school. We felt a stirring in our chests, a fizz like carbonation, like the stirring we felt when a girl let us undo the secret plastic clasp of her bra.

By now we'd adjusted to the strangeness of the empty park. Park trees looked like regular trees without the choreographed spectacle of white lights flashing along their branches. As we passed by The Big '80s Shop, we were reminded of one of our private fears. We feared our lives might be slightly less real than the lives of other boys, though we all wore the same clothes, all watched the same TV shows. Brian Furgeson, the math teacher's son, stopped to look into the shop window at stacks of colorful Italian sweaters just like the ones Bill Cosby used to wear on TV.

We were at the edge of San Francisco, yet we were at the edge of New York as well. We felt the anticipation of children as we walked by Fisherman's Wharf, a restaurant that served chowder in sourdough bowls. Mentally we were taking down all the emotional walls our parents complained about so we could absorb this experience directly. Lonnie Mason, a religious boy, removed a votive candle from his jacket pocket and rolled it along the length of his palm.

We didn't see it until we were in the preshow area. There, at the entrance, we found a tall plywood barrier. We'd seen similar barriers placed around other attractions—ones under renovation—yet we knew the San Francisco Earthquake was not under renovation. Park guests had visited it all summer. Jeff Loeb was the first to speak. "Mother fucker," he said, then walked to the barrier and punched it.

We did our best to peer inside, pressing our eyes to the dark seams between boards, but we could see very little. We saw a few bricks littering a cracked sidewalk. We saw a broken hydrant that, during park hours, gushed water. We saw the distant outline of a wooden pushcart tipped up on its side. A few of us saw a light in the telegraph office, a hanging bulb designed to swing as though the ground had just stopped shaking.

Harry Kessel suggested we push through the barrier. Brian Jenks, the track star, said we should climb over it. We were at the end of an alcove, a short hallway that, like a cattle chute, funneled guests into the broken world of San Francisco. We'd already pushed against the plywood, testing its strength. Yet we tested it again, first with our hands, then our shoulders.

We were there, at the end of the preshow area, when two security guards found us. They held their flashlights at odd angles, like the cross-eyed gaze of an idiot. We were worried, yet we were defiant as well. We felt we should look brave, if only for each other. We felt a childish lick of shame whenever a beam from their flashlights touched our bodies. We knew they would escort us outside the park, but we stayed there, our weight against the plywood barrier, longing to know what was on the other side.

It was different for all of us, the disappointment. For me it was like falling in love with a pretty girl who, in the end, turns you down for a date. For Harry Kessell it was like being first alternate for the all-state team and never getting to play. We knew our lives were changing, but didn't know how they were changing. We were juniors at a very good high school, but after watching those jets curve into the towers, we had no idea where we were going nor did we know what we should do along the way.

ACKNOWLEDGMENTS

The author would like to thank the editors of the following publications, in which some of these stories first appeared:

Fiction ("Day of the Dead"); *Georgia Review* ("Newsworld II," under the title "Newsworld"); *Indiana Review* ("Arise and Walk, Christopher Reeve"); *Mid-American Review* ("The Yoshi Compound: A Story of Post-Waco Texas"); *North American Review* ("Wrestling Al Gore"); *Seattle Review* ("The Real World"); *Sonora Review* ("Newsworld"); *Willow Springs* ("Studio Sense," under the title "Celebrity X Factor").